A Veteran's Voyage

NEWMAN SPRINGS PUBLISHING
320 Broad Street
Red Bank, NJ 07701

First originally published by Newman Springs Publishing 2020

ISBN 978-1-64801-295-2 (Paperback)
ISBN 978-1-64801-296-9 (Digital)

Printed in the United States of America

A Veteran's Voyage

A. M. BILLIOT

I n a harbor just inland of San Francisco lived an old retired Coast Guard patrol boat named *Morris*. *Morris* protected American shores for over forty years. While serving in World War II, during his late-night patrols, he would hear stories about the Navy ships that would cross the oceans to fight for our freedom. He was proud of

all the work he had done protecting his homeland but always felt if he was a little bigger, he could have gone overseas like the Navy ships. Out of all the stories he heard, the ones that stood out the most were of the battleship *Texas*. *Texas* served in World War I and II and was known for his bravery.

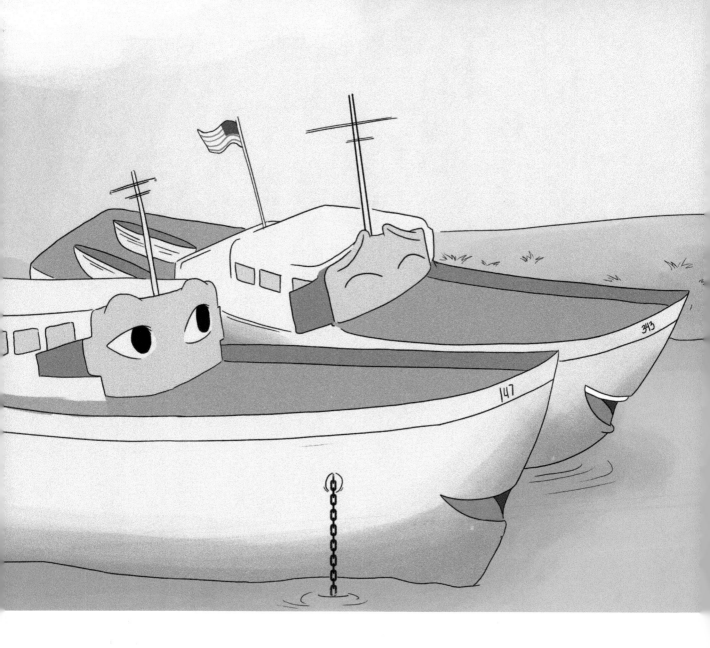

Morris spent most of his days in the harbor telling the smaller boats about his long military career. Although he enjoyed many visitors daily, in his heart he always wanted to travel the nation, visiting other war veterans to hear their tales. One day, he was telling his stories like he's done for many years when a sailboat pulled into the harbor. The sailboat listened to *Morris* tell his stories and shared some of his own. One

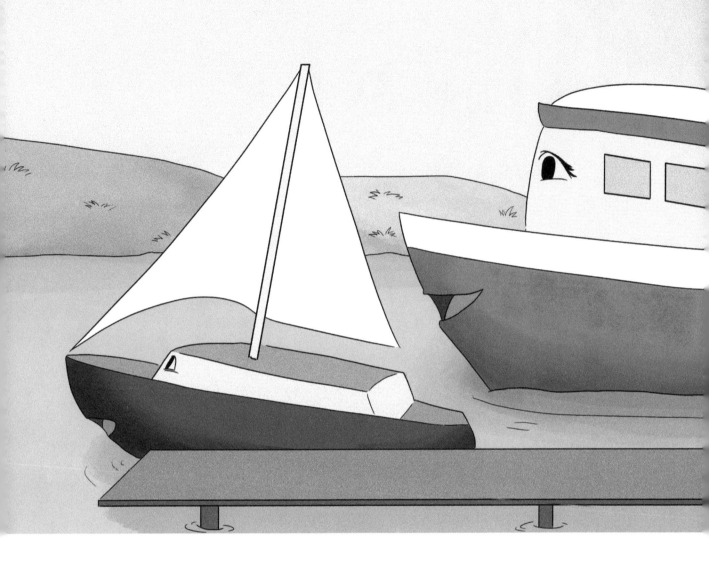

story the sailboat loved to tell was about the time he met a battleship in Houston. *Morris* instantly became excited. He was talking about the battleship *Texas*! The sailboat told *Morris* that he should take the trip to Houston and visit *Texas*. He warned *Morris* that it was a long journey, over five thousand nautical miles. *Morris* thanked the sailboat for sharing stories with him, and the sailboat continued on his way.

Weeks went by, but *Morris* could not get the thought of a new voyage out of his mind. He knew it would not be an easy trip. He was no longer the young adventurous boat he once was.

One morning he woke up and headed out on San Francisco Bay like he's done so many times before, except this time he was heading to Houston. One of his life-long dreams was about to come true. *Morris*

no longer felt like the old vessel sitting in the harbor telling tales of the good old days. He was ready to cut through the waves and get those old propellers moving again! Once he reached the Pacific Ocean, he excitedly turned south for the Panama Canal, full steam ahead! Even though *Morris* knew the trip would be difficult, he was determined to make it! Nothing would get in his way.

After seven days of traveling south in beautiful weather, his smooth sailing was coming to an end. The skies became dark, strong winds blew in, and it began to rain. The heavy winds caused rough seas. For the first time in many years *Morris* had to deal with bad weather, but this time he was all alone. *Morris* pushed forward. He knew that if

he focused and payed attention he could make it through the storm. He thought about his military training and how his teachers spent so much time preparing him to deal with tough situations. He knew that his hard work and determination would pay off. The weather stayed rough for a few more days, but he made it through.

When *Morris* finally made it to Panama, he was excited to see a different country and travel through the Panama Canal. He spent the next few days resting and meeting new boats. He told as many boats as he could about his voyage. Panama was different from anything he had ever seen. *Morris* was amazed by the variety of

cultures he was able to find in Panama. Many different vessels from all over the world travel through the canal each day. The Panama Canal connects the Pacific Ocean to the Caribbean Sea, which leads to the Atlantic Ocean. Even though he was having a great time, he knew his voyage had to continue.

Morris completed the near fifty-mile trip through the Panama Canal to the Caribbean Sea. It was a beautiful sight. He enjoyed the clear blue waters that took him north to the Gulf of Mexico. He knew that his journey was almost over. He traveled in the Gulf of Mexico

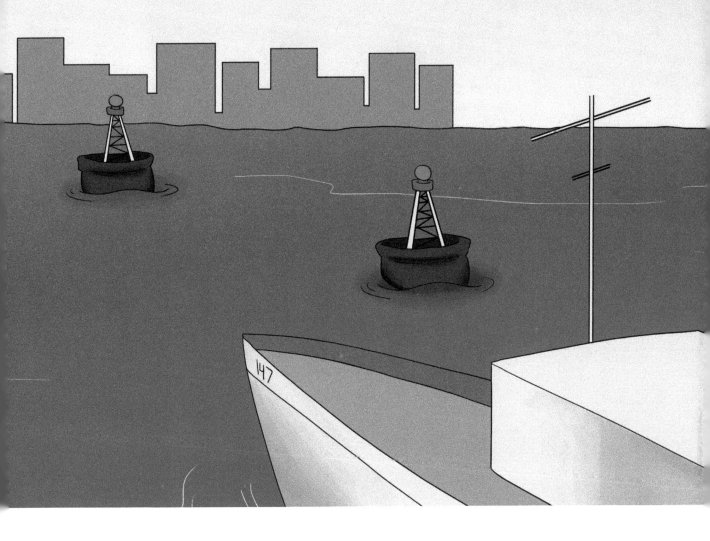

for four days, passing many oil-drilling rigs and fishing boats. This was a very different sight compared to where he began in California. He continued along toward the Houston Ship Channel. In the distance, he could see *Texas* moored at the San Jacinto Historic Site.

Morris could see a group of small boats gathered around *Texas*. He thought he must be sharing some of his exciting accounts of bravery from his past. *Texas* noticed the smaller Coast Guard patrol boat approaching from the south. When *Morris* moved closer, *Texas* could see that *Morris* was an older boat from the same era he was from. *Texas* saw his military hull number 147 painted in big bold letters on his bow. *Texas* was thrilled to see him. During his time overseas, *Texas* would hear stories of the undersized Coast Guard boats that would patrol the

coastal waters of America day and night. Those patrol boats kept his country safe while the larger ships like himself were overseas. He knew firsthand the long hours and rough waters they endured constantly. *Texas* knew that without these patrol boats, our country could not have been kept safe. He admired their bravery. He wondered how such a small boat could accomplish such a large task. Whenever *Texas* was presented with a difficult task, he thought of boats like *Morris*.

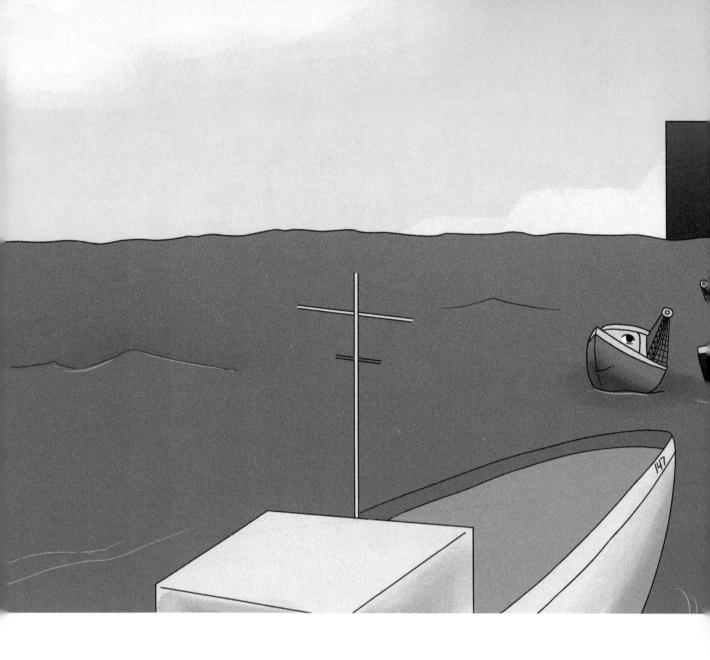

Morris was finally in front of *Texas*. Before *Morris* could say a word, *Texas* told him how he looked up to boats like him during his entire military service, the small guys that kept his family and homeland safe. *Morris* was incredibly proud that he was appreciated by such a large

and famous ship. They talked for hours that day and became friends. Before *Morris* left *Texas* thanked him for taking such a long journey so that *Texas* could finally meet a hero of his own.

You may not be the biggest or the strongest. Perhaps your job doesn't feel important compared to someone else's. Sometimes you might feel small, but you may not realize how important you are to someone else.

Work hard and be proud of who you are. Others will notice and be thankful. Though you may not see it at first, persistence and hard work will always pay off.

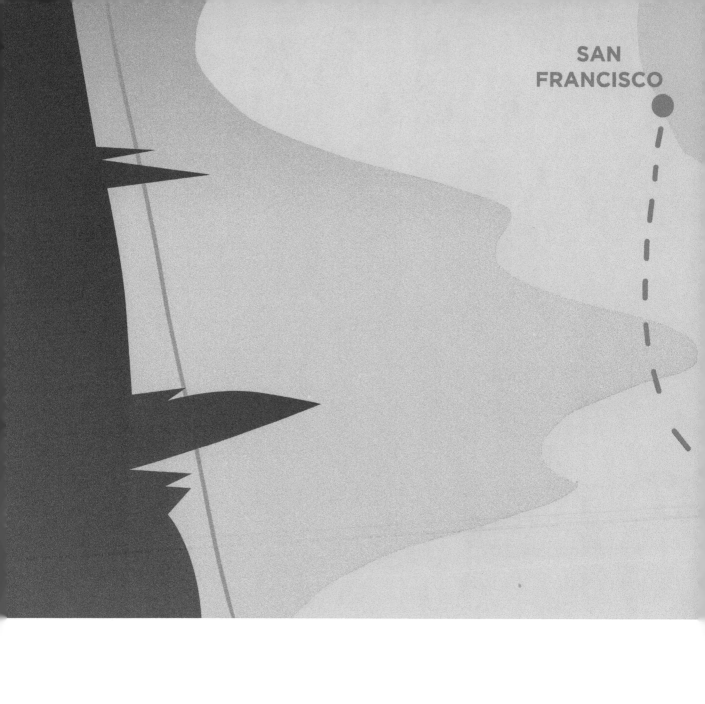

SAN
FRANCISCO

THE ANIMAL KINGDOM BOOK

Overview of the
Animal Kingdom Language Arts Program

AK PUBLISHING
P.O. Box 1736
Sebastopol, CA 95473
AKLearning@Gmail.com

© Jdanuary 22, 2024 Hulbert Martin and Amalia Kaye Martin

Color white-on-black paperback edition 8: CWB8-PB3.
Printed in the United States of America

Library of Congress Cataloging-in-Publication data
Martin, Hulbert
The Animal Kingdom Book
Overview of the Animal Kingdom (AK) Language Arts Program
/Hugh Martin and Amalia Kaye Martin
ISBN: 9798863888040
Education (Language Arts, Reading, Phonics, Elementary)
Cover design, book design, & photographs: Hugh Martin
Drawings & illustrations: Brian Narelle

HUGH MARTIN is listed in Who's Who in the United States and Who's Who in the World. Mr. Martin received his degrees and credentials from Swarthmore College, University of Pennsylvania, Indiana University, and University of California, Berkeley. He has appeared on numerous talk shows, led seminars at many colleges and corporations, and spoken at numerous professional conferences. Mr. Martin is president emeritus of the investment securities and advisory firm, Hugh Martin & Co. Hugh has a life-long interest in early-childhood education. He has been a civil rights activist, an inner-city primary grade teacher, a private school administrator, a college literature instructor, and an early-education curriculum developer.

AMALIA KAYE MARTIN ('Kaye') received her degrees and certifications from California State Fullerton and Baumann College. Kaye is an early-education specialist in the Sonoma County Public Schools, a community activist, and a member of the Occidental, CA community council. She has been a home-school coordinator and an instructor in nutrition and natural medicine at Baumann College.

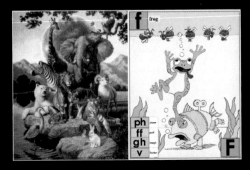

COVER & INTERIOR ILLUSTRATIONS.
Earth Animals, by James Himsworth. *The Alpha Sound Animals*, by Brian Narelle. Thanks are also given for permissions to use photos and graphics throughout this book. Some permissions pending.

THE ANIMAL KINGDOM BOOK

Overview of the
Animal Kingdom Language Arts Program

Hugh Martin

Amalia Kaye Martin

ANIMAL KINGDOM (AK) LANGUAGE ARTS

AK
PUBLISHING
Sebastopol, CA
2024

TEACHING
THE 'UNTEACHABLES'

This book is dedicated to Charletha, Verina, Kelley, Richard, Troy, Ernest, and all the other eager children in my first grade classroom at Jackie Robinson Elementary School, near the redevelopment projects in Oakland, California. Thank you to all of you for <u>teaching me</u> how young children <u>actually</u> learn to read. The Animal Kingdom Program is a testament to your infectious enthusiasm and tenacious perseverance. May life always treat you well.

This book describes a very special educational program called *Animal Kingdom (AK) Language Arts*. *Animal Kingdom* is a comprehensive language arts program that teaches children to read and write through play.

Animal Kingdom teaches through hands-on experience, fun-filled activities, and loveable animal mascots -- so it's effective with children as young as age three. *Animal Kingdom* features personalized instruction, a continuous stream of learning successes, and high-octane motivational techniques -- so the Program is also effective with older students who have been left behind by traditional classroom methods.

Every child born on this planet needs an effective introductory reading program -- so the market is huge. Yet there are few programs available that are even adequate. That's why *Animal Kingdom* represents an exceptional opportunity for both educators and publishers.

✻ **Introduction**. The poignant story of a little boy named Ronnie -- a story that shows how illiteracy destroys lives.

✻ **Education Highlights & Showcase**. Several of the most interesting and appealing Educational Features of the *Animal Kingdom* Program – first in brief Highlights, then in extended Showcase form. Shows how *Animal Kingdom* helps kids become great readers and writers.

✻ **Business Highlights**. A summary of the Program's key Business Features & Benefits. Shows how companies can achieve generous financial benefits, while doing much good for young people.

✻ **Appendix**. Books and studies by reading expert Dr. Diane McGuinness.
These substantiate and validate the principles on which *Animal Kingdom* is based.

✻ **Epilogue**. The remainder of Ronnie's heart-wrenching Story – and the hopeful lessons that can be learned from it.

THE ANIMAL KINGDOM BOOK
TABLE OF CONTENTS

Welcome to the
ANIMAL KINGDOM

INTRODUCTION

EDUCATION HIGHLIGHTS & SHOWCASE

D. Kids Become Motivated to Learn (15)

1. **The Miniature Economy**: Rewards for Every Accomplishment.
   - Showcase (38)

2. **Learning Nooks**: Secluded Alcoves for Self-Directed Learning.
   - Showcase (40)

3. **Learning Loops & Learning Ladders**: 100% Reading Success in Tiny Steps.
   - Showcase (42)

E. Teachers & Parents Guide Kids' Learning (16)

1. **Creative Tsunami**: Hugh's 20-Year Surge of Creativity & Its Surprising Results.

2. **The Peaceable Kingdom Book**: Fundamental Principles of the Seven Language Arts.
   - Showcase (46)

3. **The Kingdom of Cats Book**: Phonetic Reading in the Early Grades.

4. **The Animal Kingdom Kids of Harmony Creek** [video]. Animal Kingdom in a Charter School Kindergarten Classroom.

5. **The Many Mammals Book**: Books & Materials of AK Language Arts.

6. **The Wildlife Safari Book**: Games & Activities of AK Language Arts.

F. Adults Play Word Games Derived from Animal Kingdom (18)

1. **Skirvana Crossword Games**: Medieval Mystic Journey to Crossword Enlightenment.
   - Showcase (50)

2. **The Hidden Wisdom of Skirvana**: How to Become a Skirvana Grand Master.

3. **Skirvana in a Nutshell**: Fundamentals of the World's Greatest Word Game.

4. **Mash the Masters**: Four Grand Masters of Skirvana & How You Can Beat Them.

5. **A Beggar's Progress**: The 10 Mystic Tourneys of Skirvana [video].

G. Animal Kingdom Projects Under Development (20)

1. **Perennial Alphabet Favorites**: Converting All These to the AK Phonetic Alphabet.
   - Showcase (54)

2. **Perennial Animal Favorites**: Converting All These to the AK Alpha Animals.
   - Showcase (56)

3. **Perennial Word Game Favorites**: Converting All These to the AK Platform.
   - Showcase (58)

4. **Cartoon Friends**: Basal Readers from the Pop Culture Kids Love.

5. **Big Word Treasure Hunt**: Tons of Fun & Funny New Words from Seek & Find.
   - Showcase (60)

6. **Searchable Phonetic Dictionary**: Look Up Words by Letter, Symbol, or Sound

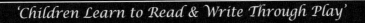

BUSINESS HIGHLIGHTS

A. How AK Improves on Other Programs (62)

Animal Kingdom improves on other language arts programs
in at least three major ways:

1. **Comprehensive, Fully-integrated Program**. Animal Kingdom teaches all seven Language Arts under a single, unified conceptual base. (62)

2. **Innovative, New Platform**. Animal Kingdom Language Arts is built on an innovative set of fundamental language arts principles that reinterpret, reinvigorate, and improve traditional methods of reading and language arts instruction. (63)

3. **Fresh, New Hands-on Learning Methods**. The Animal Kingdom Program is built on a fresh, new foundation of kid-friendly learning methods -- techniques where the joy and excitement of play is combined with a continuous stream of learning successes. (65)

B. An Opportunity for Educators & Publishers (66)

Animal Kingdom represents an exceptional opportunity for educators and publishers in at least four ways:

1. **People + Profit: A Win-Win Opportunity**. The Animal Kingdom Program presents a true win-win opportunity: A reading and language program that can do much good for America's children -- yet offers generous rewards for innovative educators and publishers. (66)

2. **Diverse Markets & Learning Environments**. Because of its unique approach to learning, the Animal Kingdom Program is adaptable to at least a dozen different educational markets and learning environments. (68)

3. **Diverse Modes of Production**. Animal Kingdom consists of many different kinds of learning products -- reading books, manuals, tangible learning materials, toys, board games, software, online educational and gaming sites, etc. -- each with its own set of publishing and manufacturing opportunities. (70)

4. **Diverse Channels of Distribution**. Some Animal Kingdom books and materials will be distributed directly through school systems; others through retail book stores; others through toy and game stores; still others through on-line networks. (71)

APPENDIX & EPILOGUE

1. **Validation for Animal Kingdom**. Scholarly and popular studies from reading expert, Dr. Diana McGuinness. Confirms the validity and effectiveness of the principles upon which the Animal Kingdom Program is built. (72)

2. **Ronnie's Story: How It Played Out.** The tragic conclusion to Ronnie's story. And the hopeful lessons we can learn from it. (73)

DEATH AT AN EARLY AGE:
How Our Schools Create Losers in the Game of Life

This is the story of **Ronnie* -- a boy with his fair share of advantages, whose life was ruined just because he never learned to read**. Ronnie's story begins over thirty years ago, but is even more true for kids today.

FAMILY HAVEN IN A GHETTO JUNGLE

It's true that Ronnie grew up in the **notorious West Oakland ghetto**, just across the Bay from San Francisco. But, unlike many other boys in his neighborhood, Ronnie had a **live-in dad** (Fernando) with a steady job driving the Fruitvale bus for Oakland Transit. And a **stay-home mama** (Makayla), who made Ronnie a hot breakfast each morning, and a sack lunch before he left for class. By the time Ronnie came back from school, Makayla had returned from after her half-day cleaning job in the posh Piedmont hills, and was there to greet him with a warm hug and tasty snack.

Both Fernando and Makayla came from families that were largely illiterate. However, through dedication and hard work, they had raised themselves to at least **functional literacy** -- and had much higher aspirations for their darling boy. Fernando and Makayla had a **happy, stable marriage** -- despite the difficulties of **melding Makayla's Black background with Fernando's Hispanic family**. Although they had wanted more children, Fernando and Makayla were able to produce only one child -- so they **lavished all their hopes and affections on little Ronnie**.

Despite his **parents' limited incomes**, Ronnie was always dressed in clean, mended shirts; was fed healthy meals hot off the stove; and was given **his own private sleeping alcove**, with a comfortable, warm pullout bed, surrounded by his favorite hot-wheel cars and stuffed animal figures. On weekends, **Fernando and Makayla often took Ronnie on outings** -- to Children's Fairyland on Lake Merritt; or to the petting center at the Oakland Zoo; or to the Little Farm and pony rides at Berkeley's nearby Tilden Park.

Fernando and Makayla did their best to care for Ronnie's mind and spirit as well. Even when they were tired from work, the family attended **the big, throbbing Abyssinian Apostolic Church** down on Broadway -- where Makayla in a pink satin robe sang choir, and Fernando in his one good suit took the offering. They limited Ronnie's TV to wholesome shows like Sesame Street and Muppets. They cuddled with Ronnie at night, while reading him *The Little Engine That Could*, just before he drifted into a peaceful sleep. They even **tried to give Ronnie a head start in reading** -- teaching him the alphabet and the letter sounds from the *Big Bird Alphabet Book* they bought at Costco. **Up until his first day at his new school, Ronnie's prospects for life seemed pretty bright...** [continued on page 73]

A LIFE ON THE EDGE

Ronnie was a good kid from a good home. How could something as simple as a mediocre reading program have caused Ronnie's life to crash and burn? And how can we prevent that from happening to the next generation of Ronnie's? **To read the rest of Ronnie's tragic story (and the hopeful lessons we can learn from it), please turn to page 73.**

[* Ronnie's story is a composite of several typical, true-life stories -- drawn from the author's personal experience -- as well as that of other writers, such as Jonathan Kozol, who have spent their lives amidst such conditions. The title of this section is borrowed from Kozol's classic book of that name.]

ANIMAL KINGDOM EDUCATION HIGHLIGHTS

Animal Kingdom Language Arts is a comprehensive educational program that teaches children to read and write through play. The Animal Kingdom Program consists of several dozen books, educational materials, and other products. In this Highlights Section of our Overview, we show several of the Program's most valuable and appealing Highlights – in each of seven categories: A. **Learning the Alpha Sounds** (10). B. **Combining the Alpha Sounds** (12). C. **Writing Stories** (14). D. **Motivational Techniques** (15). E. **Materials for teachers and parents** (16). F. **Adult games** (18). And G. **Products Under Development** (20).

Among those Highlights are several important 'Gateway' Products -- especially appealing 'Marquee' Products that introduce teachers and parents to the unique benefits of the Program. In the Showcase section (22), we describe in greater detail many of those Gateway Products.[1]

In the Business Section (62), we will then summarize the Program's major features and benefits, and show why Animal Kingdom represents an exceptional opportunity for both educators and publishers.

A. *Kids Learn the Alpha Sounds*

The most fundamental principle of Animal Kingdom: The Phonetic Alphabet. Traditional Alphabet Books present just the 26 Letters of the Alphabet -- and imply that there are just 26 Sounds that correspond to those Letters ('**a** is for **apple**'). But *the English language actually uses 43 different Sounds* -- along with various Letters (and combinations of Letters) that represent those Sounds. These 43 Sounds are the basis for what AK calls the 'Phonetic Alphabet.' *When children are taught the Phonetic Alphabet, there are almost no 'irregulars,' no 'exceptions,' no 'special rules,' and no confusing inconsistencies. As a result, there is virtually no dyslexia*: Children learn to read quickly, easily, and at an early age.

43 Alpha Animals of the Real Alphabet. Built not on the faulty, 26-Letter Traditional Alphabet, but on the complete 43-Sound Phonetic Alphabet. Each [Alph]a Sound' is associated with a cute and loveable 'Alpha Animal' -- an animal [whos]e name begins with (or includes) that particular Sound. ('*Monkey*' begins [with ']*mmm.*') Naturalistic stories that introduce each of the 43 Alpha Sounds [thro]ugh its respective Alpha Animal: The Animal's name, what it looks like, where [it liv]es, what it likes to eat, what it likes to do. In the process, children learn [the S]ound (and the corresponding Letters) that each Animal represents.

Highlight A2. SILLY STORIES FOR ALPHA SOUNDS >>
Dr. Seuss-Style Stories for All 43 Alpha Animals. As with An[imal] Adventures, this book introduces children to the 43 Alpha Animal[s] and to the Sound and Letters that each Animal represents. This [book] with: Zany, Dr. Seuss-like stories that use alliteration and rhymin[g] sensitize children to the 43 Alpha Sounds as they are heard in sp[oken] language. Shows kids that language can be interesting and

[1] Those Gateway Products are linked to the Showcase Section with a Forward Symbol (>>) and page number.

Highlight A3. ALPHA BABIES ANIMAL FIGURES >> 3

Cuddly Beanie Babies for All 43 Alpha Sounds. Loveable, cuddly, little 'Beanie Baby' animal friends that represent the 43 Sounds of the English language. Each animal is tagged with a charming miniature storybook -- a tiny book that tells either the Animal Adventure or the Silly Story for that particular Animal. Familiarizes the child with each Animal, creates a bond of affection, and affixes the Animal's name and its Alpha Sound securely in a child's memory.

Highlight A4. MY ALPHA SOUND ANIMALS:
Sound/Symbol Cards and Charts
for Phonetic Reading and Spelling

The Keystone of the AK Program.
The keystone of any good Phonics program is the series of 43 Sounds that comprise the English Language -- along with Letters and Symbols that represent those Sounds. This book presents two complete sets of 43 Sound/Symbol Cards (one beginning, one advanced) -- showing each Alpha Animal, along with its corresponding Alpha Sound and Alpha Symbols. Included also are two Charts of all 43 together – as well as descriptions and explanations of the underlying principles and processes of Phonetic Reading. The fundamental resource for all Phonics activities.

Highlight A5. ALPHA ANIMAL BLANKET

Wrapped in Alpha Animals from Their Earliest Years. All 43 Alpha Animals and their Alpha Symbols on a fleecy, cozy blanket you can wrap around your child from their earliest years of life. And later hang in their bedroom as a wall decoration and reading reference. Kids will begin learning Animal Kingdom spontaneously, as soon as they're able to talk!

B. Kids Combine the Alpha Sounds To Form Words & Syllables

Once a child learns the 43 Alpha Sounds and their associated Symbols, he/she needs lots of practice translating those Letters into Words. AK's *Phonetic Blocks* makes this 'decoding' and 'blending' process easy -- with fast-paced, exciting games that are fun to play. When selected Blocks are rolled like dice and arranged in the proper order, *they form virtually every pronounceable syllable in the English language.* When games are sequenced from easiest to hardest S– and combined with Symbol Strips (*Six Wild Cats*, below) -- t*hey enable a child to read a representative assortment of over 353,000 words and syllables!*

ghlight B1. PHONETIC BLOCKS >> 32

er 353,000 Words & Syllables from 1

ocks. With this set of 13 color-coded Let
ocks, kids practice a representative assort
over 353,000 Words and Syllables -- virt
ery pronounceable Syllables in the English
age. Motivation remains high -- with fast
ced, exciting games that give children tons
ccess with the basic skills of Phonetic Rea

The Playing Field of the AK Program.
An enclosed space where kids can arrange their Blocks
ile playing *Phonetic Blocks* games. For reference, the
at displays a chart of all the Alpha Animals and their
ols, as well as composites of all three types of Sylla-

LEOPARD PATTERNS
Short Vowel Syllable Patterns

TIGER PATTERNS
Long Vowel Syllable Patterns

LION PATTERNS
Double-Letter Vowel Syllable Patterns

Highlight B3. THE SIX WILD CATS BOOK:
Symbol Strips for Phonetic Reading

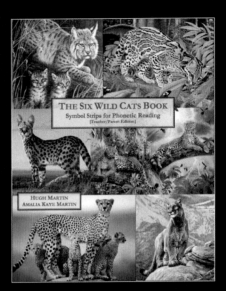

A Set of Virtual Blocks. A Symbol Strip is like a Phonetic
Block where all six sides have been laid out in a vertical column
– and where Symbols are chosen by the roll of a Number Block.
Symbol Strips can be used in place of Blocks in many Phonetic
Blocks games. Strips have several advantages over Blocks – because they cover many: 1) Rare and unusual Symbols; 2) Difficult
or confusing Symbols; 3) Unusual Operators; and 4) Double Consonants. This book shows all the Symbol Strips of the AK Program,
arranged in the proper sequence from easiest to most complex.
It is like having 56 additional Phonetic Blocks to play with.

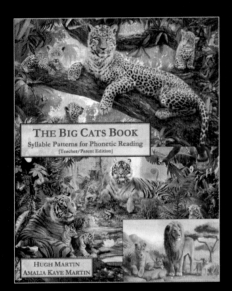

ighlight B4. THE BIG CATS BOOK:
yllable Patterns for Phonetic Reading

he 24 Patterns for 353,000 Syllables.
he pronunciation of the Vowels in a given word is affecte
e arrangement of Vowels and Consonants in that word.
rrangement is called a Pattern. This book contains all 2
owel-Consonant Syllable Patterns -- six for Short Vowel
r Long Vowels, and nine for Double-Letter Vowels. The
ession through a particular set of Patterns is called a P
rn Journey. This book leads children through all three
rn Journeys. In the course of these Journeys, kids will
representative assortment of every pronounceable Sylla
r language -- over 353,000 Words and Syllables in all!

Highlight B5. STAR POWER FOR BIG CATS:
Study Plans & Progress Reports
for Phonetic Reading

The Game Plan for Phonetic Reading.
This companion to *The Big Cats Book* (above) leads
teachers and students through a complete sequence of
Pattern Journeys. It also gives kids and their teachers a way to keep track of their progress and to cele-

C. Kids Compose Stories from the Alpha Sounds

BABOONS BY THE BEACH
It's a bright, beautiful day at the beach with blue skies and billowing clouds as a boat passes below a biplane pulling a banner of bottles while a bunch of baboons in berets bury bones, play banjo, and balance on beach balls, as a box of bananas floats by.

Highlight C1. SILLY STORIES FROM ALPHA LAND >>
Zany, One-Sentence Stories for Each of the Alpha Sound
Goofy stories just one sentence long, each containing lots of w
beginning with a particular Alpha Sound. With the teacher's (
parent's) help, kids search a busy illustration for words that b
with a given Sound. Then the teacher reads the story out loud
while the child points the parts of the picture where the word
the story are found. A great way to give kids inspiration for

Highlight
ITE YOUR OWN SILLY STORIES! >>
the Words Kids Need to Write Their O
s compose their own crazy *Silly Stories* (A
ng a list of words that begin with a partic
Sound. Then kids draw their own goofy il
tration on the facing p
Companion to *Alpha Land Stories* (ab

MY OWN SILLY STORIES

Cosmo and His Friends
Make up your own Silly-Story about Cosmo the Cat, his family, and his friends.
Here are some good ccc-words:
- Cosmo's family: **Cosmo, Claudia, Casper, and Calypso.**
- Cosmo's friends: **Cordelia the Camel, Clifton the Caterpillar, Casimir the Crab, Kerwin the Koala Bear, and Katrina the Kangaroo.**
- Other animals: **chameleon, cobra, cow, clownfish, cockatoo, cockroach, crow, cod, condor, cougar, coyote, crane, cricket, crocodile.**
- Other Names: **Calvert, Cato, Clancy, Cuthbert, Kirby, Callista, Camille, Crystal, Clementine.**
- Name-words: **cabin, camp, candle, cap, car, carrot, castle, claw, clock, cliff, clothes, cloud, clown, coat, coconut, coffee, color, computer, corner, crown, cub, cup, king, kitchen, kite, school.**
- Action-words: **carry, catch, clap, claw, climb, cook, count, crawl, cry, cut, kiss.**
- Describing-words: **cold, cuddly, kind.**
- Helping verbs: **can.**

D. Kids Become Motivated to Learn

Rewards for Every Accomplishment. A classroom motivational system that that uses a child-size, grassroots economy to encourage kids to work hard and do well. Kids earn 'play money' for their accomplishments, save up their money in a personal 'bank,' compose a 'shopping list' of preferred purchases, buy 'prizes' with their earnings, and celebrate their achievements together in a weekly 'party.' Much like our adult economy, the Miniature Economy provides a comprehensive and effective motivational structure for a whole range of classroom activities.

hlight D2. Learning Nooks >> 40
luded Spaces for Self-Directed Learning.
fortable, secluded alcoves in corners of the classroom –
here spontaneous, non-structured, self-directed learning
exploration can take place without distraction. Sepa-
d from the bustle of the classroom, kids can explore
activity of their choice -- including Stories, Language,
nals, Building, Art, Science, Role Playing, and Playing
cher. Since kids must first complete their seatwork be-
migrating to a Learning Nook, they are motivated to
h their assigned tasks quickly and accurately.

& LEARNING LADDER >> 42

100% Success in Tiny Steps. Simple but highly-structured techniques of 'programmed instruction' – that teach any child Rote Learning Skills (like Phonetic Reading or Arithmetic Computation) by 'programming' the child's mind to 'think like a computer.' In each Round of the *Learning Loop*, a child proceeds through several tiny, easily-learned Steps – leading to the mastery of a particular Skill. With the *Learning Ladder*, that child rises through several tiny, easily-attained *Learning Loops* – leading to the mastery of a whole set of Skills. Those Skills then become so routine and automatic that they function in the background – freeing the child's mind for more creative activities, like Reading for Meaning and Writing for Expression.

Learning Ladder
Developing Thinking Skills in Young Kids

Rachana Misra

E. Teachers & Parents Guide Kids' Learning

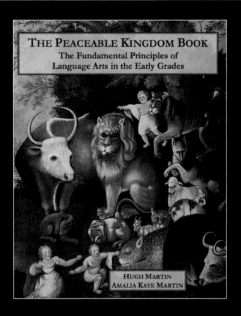

THE PEACEABLE KINGDOM BOOK
The Fundamental Principles of
Language Arts in the Early Grades

HUGH MARTIN
AMALIA KAYE MARTIN

hlight E1. THE PEACEABLE KINGDOM BOOK:
ndamental Principles of Language Arts
the Early Grades >> 46

Crown Jewel of the AK Program. A comprehensive
rview of the Fundamental Principles of all seven Languag
s – along with the instructional methods and materials
ded to implement those Principles. Clear explanations
teaching methods for each Language Art: Phonetic Read
Vocabulary & Comprehension, Spelling, Grammar, Hand-

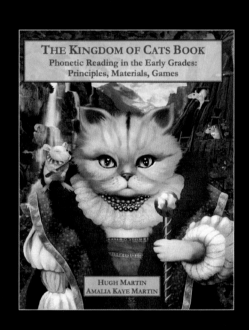

THE KINGDOM OF CATS BOOK
Phonetic Reading in the Early Grades:
Principles, Materials, Games

HUGH MARTIN
AMALIA KAYE MARTIN

Phonetic Reading in the Early Grad
-- Principles, Materials, and Metho

The Flagship of the AK Program. A detailed
scription of the AK Phonetic Reading Program – w
emphasis on Phonetic Blocks [B1). All the Princip
Materials, and Methods you'll need to teach Phone
Reading successfu

CTW
SESAME STREET

ghlight E3. THE ANIMAL KINGDOM KIDS
HARMONY CREEK (video)

imal Kingdom in a Charter School Kindergarten.
w a freeform version of the AK Program stimulates
arning in a charter school kindergarten classroom.
is charming, little homebrew video shows it all: The
s, the classroom, the playground, the teeth! Pho-
tic blocks, the Miniature Economy, the Learning
oks, the Learning Loop, the books and materials.

THE MANY MAMMALS BOOK
Animal Kingdom (AK) Language Arts
Materials Manual

Highlight E4. THE MANY MAMMALS BOOK:
Books & Materials of the AK Language Arts Program

The Treasure Chest of the AK Program. Detailed descriptions of the dozens of materials included in the Animal Kingdom Program, with complete specifications. Shows the relative importance of each material, its location in the full program, and its current state of development.

THE WILDLIFE SAFARI BOOK
Animal Kingdom (AK) Language Arts
Games and Activities Manual

Highlight E5. THE WILDLIFE SAFARI BOOK
**Games & Activities
for the AK Language Arts Program**

The Playbook of the AK Program. Detailed instructions and illustrations for playing all the games and activities in the Animal Kingdom Program -- except for *Phonetic Blocks* and Phonetic Reading. (See *Kingdom of Cats*, E2.)

F. Adults Play Word Games Derived from Animal Kingdom

Animal Kingdom isn't just for kids. The same AK Principles can be applied to numerous language games and activities for older children and adults. The ultimate word game for conversion to the AK Platform is the greatest of all word game classics, *Scrabble*.

Medieval Mystic Journey to Crossword Enlightenment. AK's *Skirvana* is a radical improvement and revitalization of the world's most popular word game, *Scrabble*. Rather than just a single game, *Skirvana* is a nested series of <u>ten</u> crossword games -- where each game builds on the last and adds one new feature. *Skirvana* offers numerous forms of strategy not available in *Scrabble*, and avoids *Scrabble's* many limitations – including boring waits and playing board congestion. At the simpler levels, SKIRVANA is great reading, spelling, and vocabulary practice for children. At the most advanced levels, *Skirvana* will challenge the word skills of even the most dedicated *Scrabble* fanatic.

Secrets of Becoming a Skirvana Grand Master

All the Rules, Materials, & Strategies of *Skirvana*.
Skirvana is a major improvement on the world-famous crossword game, *Scrabble*. In *Skirvana*, players evolve through ten Circles of Initiation, from lowly Scrabble Serf to exalted Grand Master – attaining the nirvana-like state of language enlightenment called Skirvana. This big book explains all the rules, the materials, and the strategies you will need to become an expert in this challenging and revolutionary board game.

Highlight F3. SKIRVANA IN A NUTSHELL: All the Essentials of the World's Greatest Word Game

The Quickstart Version of *Hidden Wisdom*. All the basics of this complex series of games – in a simple, entertaining format: Principles, Games, Materials, Rules, and Strategies – along with broader significance of the game. A brief and entertaining condensation of our rules and

How Four Grand Masters of Skirvana Play the Game – and How You Can Beat Them

Beat the Masters at Their Own Game. A series of simulated, high-level game situations – where you can experience what it's like to play a high-level game of *Skirvana*. We challenge you to test your skills in a contest against four *Skirvana* Grand Masters – the super-heroes **A**chilles, **B**oudicca, **C**onan, and **D**artha. Before each play is made, we show you the Gameboard as it stands, along with the Tiles on a given Master's rack. We then challenge you to use those Tiles to devise the highest-scoring play you can come up with. Once you've taken your best shot, we show you what word was actually played by that Master. Were you able to 'Mash the Master?' What did the Master teach you about playing the game?

The Mystic Tourneys of Skirvana (video)

The Fantasy Narrative Behind *Skirvana*. How Adam, a hapless beggar on the streets of Medieval England, progresses up the ranks of England's highly-stratified society – merely by becoming a Master of a fascinating new crossword game, called *Skirvana*. This charming, little home-brew video shows the fantasy narrative behind the game. By transforming *Skirvana* from a mere word game into a dramatic personal journey, this this intriguing storyline will ignite popular en-

G. *A̶̶n̶i̶m̶a̶l̶ ̶K̶i̶n̶g̶d̶o̶m̶ ̶P̶r̶o̶j̶e̶c̶t̶ ̶U̶n̶d̶e̶r̶* Development

Highlight G1. PERENNIAL ALPHABET FAVORITES >> 54

verting Traditional Alphabet Books & Toys to the Phonetic abet. An entire industry has been built around a vast array of roducts that teach children the Letters of the Alphabet. These *Perennial Alphabet Favorites* include: Alphabet books, alphabet ks, alphabet puzzles, etc. As explained on page 22, such mate- ls are tragically misleading – because they indoctrinate children the major cause of childhood dyslexia, the Traditional Alphabet. naximize every child's chances for reading success, Animal King- m is converting each of these products from the faulty and mis- ading 26-Letter Traditional Alphabet to AK's 43-Sound Phonetic habet. These Phonetic Alphabet products will have a receptive dience, since they are derived from time-tested books, toys, and es that parents and teachers already know and trust. They will end to supplant Traditional Alphabet products, because they are demonstrably more effective in teaching reading.

Highlight G2. PERENNIAL ANIMAL FAVORITES >> 56

Converting Traditional Animal Toys & Books to the Alpha mals. Another entire industry has been built around the vast of products that capitalize on a child's innate love of animals. These *Perennial Animal Favorites* include animal figures, books, and games that are popular year-after-year with each succeed generation of children. Such products are appealing to publishe and toy manufacturers, because they will always have a ready ket – as each new cohort of young animal-lovers comes of age. mal Kingdom is converting these Animal Favorites into effective learning materials, in two ways: First, by assembling sets of 43 pha Animals, representing the 43 Sounds of the Phonetic Alpha And second, by including some enhancement that enables a child derive that Animal's Alpha Sound from its name. For instance,

erting Popular Word Games to the AK Platform. A third en- re industry has been built around the vast array of products that alize on the public's fascination with Word Games. We call these cts *Perennial Word Game Favorites* – Letter Games, Word Games, hmar Games, Game Books, and other play materials that are popu- r year-after-year, with each succeeding generation of both adults children. Games like: *Scrabble, Spill-&-Spell, Bananagrams, Book- worm, Mad Libs,* and so forth. Animal Kingdom is converting these ord Game Favorites to the AK Platform -- both for recreation and earning. Such games are appealing to publishers and game manu-

Highlight G4. CARTOON FRIENDS

Kid-Friendly Basal Readers from Pop Culture. Most present-day basal reading materials for young students are little better than the old *Dick and Jane* books -- dull and insipid, both in their lame stories and in their pallid illustrations. Why not teach children to read using the fun characters and stories they already know and love? Why not let Donald Duck and Bugs Bunny be their teachers? Or Snoopy and Miss Piggy? Or Luke Skywalker and Frodo Baggins? Or Pinocchio and Snow White? Or Calvin and Hobbes? *Cartoon Friends* teaches kids to read their favorite cartoons and comic strips -- like *Peanuts* and *Calvin & Hobbes*. As well as their favorite books and movies -- like *Alice in Wonderland* and *Harry Potter*. Such illustrated stories are now available as cartoon anthologies, as 'Classics-Illustrated'-style comic books, and as pic-

Highlight G5. BIG WORD TREASURE HUNT >> 60

Fun & Funny New Words from Seek-and-Find. A series of fun vocabulary builders, derived from popular and beloved 'Seek-and-Find' books. Like Martin Handford's *Where's Waldo?* And Richard Scarry's *What Do People Do All Day?* In the AK version, kids pore over a crowded, comic scene in a kind of Scavenger Hunt -- where they 'collect' a long list of 'Treasures' (new words), then trade them in for 'Prize Money' from the Miniature Economy. As kids search each oversize page of these fascinating books, they discover dozens of fun and funny

Highlight G6. SEARCHABLE PHONETIC DICTIONARY

Look Up Words by Letter, Symbol, or Sound. In order to look up a word's spelling in a conventional dictionary, we must first know how it's spelled – but that is the very thing we are trying to find out! Likewise, when we want to look up a word's definition, we must first know how that word is spelled – but often we only know how it sounds. (When we want to find the spelling or the definition for a word that sounds like '*fonee*,' how would we know to look under '*phony*'?) *** This essential reference work will enable *Skirvana* players to look up a word -- not just by its Letters -- but by its multi-letter Alpha Symbols (like *ch*, *sh*, and *ea*). And by their corresponding Alpha Sounds (like the initial Sounds of *chipmunk*, *shark*, and *eagle*). Thus, *Skirvana* players can more easily devise monster new words from the Alpha-Tiles on their rack. *** Our Phonetic Dictionary will also tend to displace traditional dictionaries for general use – since it is the first reference work to bridge that critical

Animal Kingdom Language Arts
SHOWCASE OF GATEWAY PRODUCTS

Among the many products highlighted in the previous section are several 'Gateway' or 'Marquee' Products – especially appealing products that introduce students and teachers to the unique benefits of the AK Program. This section showcases AK Gateway Products in seven categories: A. **Learning the Alpha Sounds** (22). B. **Combining the Alpha Sounds** (32). C. **Writing Stories** (34). D. **Motivational Techniques** (38). E. **Materials for teachers and parents** (46). F. **Adult games** (50). And G. **Products Under Development** (54).

A. KIDS LEARN THE ALPHA SOUNDS

In order to read phonetically, a child must learn the '**Phonetic Alphabet**' -- the 43 Sounds of the English language, and their associated Letters and Symbols. We first introduce this Phonetic Alphabet and explain why it's important. We then showcase three products that teach various aspects of this Alphabet: *Animal Adventures* (26), *Silly Stories* (28), and *Alpha Babies* (30).

Animal Adventures

MIRANDA THE MONKEY
Miranda the mischievous Monkey lives in the dense rain forest jungle. Miranda likes to pick tender fruit at night from her favorite tip-top branch.

Perennial Alphabet Favorites

Silly Stories

Phonetic Blocks

Alpha Babies

Silly Stories from Alpha Land

THE BULL BY THE BARN
A bear with a book bag, bending a bar,
rides a bike backwards past a barn
where a big blue bull in a bad mood is

Skirvana Crossword Game

Big Word Treasure Hunt

INTRODUCTION: *A New Kind of Alphabet*

In many cases, the first learning book that you as a parent will buy for your child is an **Alphabet Book**. Of course, the Alphabet Book introduces your child to the Letters of the Alphabet. But more important, through accompanying pictures, this Alphabet Book supposedly shows your child how those Letters are pronounced when reading. The Letter **A** is pronounced like the first sound in **Apple**. The Letter **B** is pronounced like the first sound in **Ball**. And so forth. *This traditional Alphabet Book implies that, when your child learns all those Letters and their respective Sounds, he/she will then be equipped with the basic skill needed to read.*

The Traditional Alphabet: Our Kids' Biggest Reading Problem

Unfortunately, that's where the problems begin. *There are only 26 Letters in the Alphabet. Yet there are a total of 43 distinct Sounds in the English Language.* What happens to those other 17 Sounds? How are they pronounced? What Letter, or combination of Letters, represents them on the printed page? Can there be two or more different Sounds that are represented by the same Letter? Can there be two or more Letters that represent the same Sound?

This mismatch between the 26 Letters and the 43 Sounds is the source of serious confusion for young readers. According to reading expert Diane McGuinness,[2] *this discrepancy alone is the major cause of Dyslexia among problem readers.* Even for successful readers, the Traditional Alphabet necessitates a myriad of complicated 'Irregulars' and 'Exceptions' that a child must learn through 'Special Rules' and slogans: '**I** before **e**, except after **c**.' 'When two vowels go walking, the first does the talking.' And so forth.

CHESTER THE CHATTERY CHIPMUNK
Chester the chubby,
chattery chipmunk
cheers for chewy
cheddar cheese.
Chomp, chomp
go his cheeks!

Ch

Missing Sounds. The Traditi[onal] [Al]phabet covers only 26 of the [S]ounds of the English langua[ge]. [Th]e Consonant-Sounds for *ch*, [s]h, and *ng* are missing. Likew[ise] [th]e Vowel-Sounds for *aw, ow,* and *oy* are also missing.

The Myth of Dyslexia
Summarizing the extensive research on Dyslexia, reading expert Dr. Diane McGuinness concludes: "There is no evidence from any of these studies that most poor readers have anything wrong with them, except the inability to read an alphabetic writing system . . ." In other words, most students with supposed 'reading disorders' will be 'cured' when they are taught a <u>complete</u> Alphabet consisting of <u>all</u> the Sounds and Symbols

A Scientific Revolution in Reading

Why Our Children **Can't Read** *And What We Can Do About It*

Diane McGuinness, Ph.D.

[2] See Validation for AK Principles (70).

The New Alphabet:
The Best Solution to Our Kids' Reading Problems

The books and materials in this section present a new kind of Alphabet – an Alphabet of 43 Letters, or combinations of Letters ('Alpha Symbols'), that correspond exactly to the 43 Sounds of the English Language (the 'Alpha Sounds'). Moreover, the Symbols of this Alphabet are illustrated with pictures of beloved 'Alpha Animals' – Animals whose names begin with (or end with, or include) those Sounds.

Through appealing illustrations and engaging stories, each child learns an interesting lesson or story about each Alpha Animal. Through simple games and exercises, each child also learns to derive each Animal's Sound from its name: '**Bear** begins with **bbb**!'; '**Cat** begins with **ccc**!'; '**Chipmunk** begins with **chchch**!'. And so forth. *These stories and exercises encourage a child to enjoy and bond strongly with each Animal. As a result, each Animal's corresponding Symbol and Sound becomes securely embedded in each child's mind.*

MY ALPHA-SOUND ANIMALS
[Primary Symbols]

No Missing Letters. AK's Phonetic Alphabet contains all 43 Sounds of the English Language -- along with all of their associated Letters and Symbols.

Teaching the Phonetic Alphabet: Books and Materials

The two 'Alphabet books' in this section -- *Animal Adventures* and *Silly Stories* -- both cover the same basic lessons about the Phonetic Alphabet. *Animal Adventures* (26) emphasizes the natural life of each Alpha Animal, while *Silly Stories* (28) focuses on the particular Sound represented by that Animal. With both books, each child learns all the Sounds of our Language, along with all the Symbols that represent those Sounds. Both *Animal Adventures* and *Silly Stories* also come in the form of *Alpha Babies* (30) – adorable little stuffed animals similar to *Beanie Babies*, each with its own miniature storybook for that particular Animal.

❀ *Animal Adventures*, *Silly Stories*, and *Alpha Babies* are prime examples of what AK calls *Perennial Alphabet Favorites* (54). A Perennial Favorite is a familiar, much-loved product (like the traditional 26-Letter Alphabet Book), that AK converts to the phonetically-correct 43-Sound Phonetic Alphabet.

❀ Other Highlights described in this book are also conversions of Perennial Favorites. *Phonetic Blocks* (32), for instance, are color-coded 'Alphabet Blocks' which combine in various patterns to form virtually every pronounceable word or syllable in the English Language.

❀ Once the child learns to sound out words phonetically, he/she can then move on to reading's greatest pleasure -- the Whole Language skills of Vocabulary & Comprehension. For starters, AK teaches these skills in four ways: Through an innovative set of basal readers, called *Cartoon Friends* (20). A series of vocabulary-building seek-and-find books, called *Big Word Treasure Hunt* (60). A set of crazy stories featuring a single Alpha Sound, called *Silly Stories from Alpha Land* (34). And a challenging, Scrabble-like crossword game, called *Skirvana* (50). *With these skills, each child has access to a vast array of fascinating books, understands and enjoys these books, and embarks on a lifelong reading adventure.*

Cartoon Friends

THE LION KING

THE THREE KEY TERMS

The following three terms are fundamental to understanding the Animal Kingdom Program:

✤ **Alpha Sound** (also called 'Sound' or 'Phoneme')
One of the 43 Phonetic Sounds we use to form words in Spoken English.

> Ex: The word **cat** contains three Alpha Sounds – the Sounds /c/, /a/, and /t/.

✤ **Alpha Symbol** (also called 'Symbol' or 'Grapheme')
A letter or combination of letters we use to represent a single Alpha Sound.

> Ex: The word **cat** contains three Alpha Symbols – the letters **c**, **a**, and **t**. The words **ch-a-t** and **c-augh-t** also have just three Alpha Symbols, even though they both have more than three letters.

✤ **Alpha Animal** (also called 'Animal')
An animal whose name begins with (or ends with, or includes) a particular Alpha Sound.

> Ex: The three animals **cat**, **alligator**, and **tiger** were chosen as AK's Alpha Animals for the Sounds in the word **c-a-t** – because their names begin with the Sounds /c/, /a/, and /t/.

Alpha Sound
('Sound')

Alpha Sounds A1. ALPHA SOUND ANIMAL ADVENTURES:
The 43 Alpha Animals of the Real Alphabet

When a little child first encounters the outside world, one of his/her greatest delights is the world of animals. A child's first great adventures are often to the Petting Zoo or the Little Farm. Thus, many of the first words a child learns are names of beloved animals -- doggie, kitty, horsie, piggie, teddy, and so forth. The Animal Kingdom Program capitalizes on a child's innate love of animals, by teaching children to derive the 43 Alpha Sounds from an assortment of loveable and fascinating Alpha Animals. *Alpha Sound Animal Adventures* is the child's first Alphabet Book. It introduces children to the Alpha Animals -- along with two other bedrock concepts: the Alpha Sounds and the Alpha Symbols.

✸ **The Naturalistic Alpha Animals.** *Animal Adventures* uses naturalistic stories and illustrations to acquaint the child with each Alpha Animal -- its appearance, its personality, where it lives, what it likes to do, what it likes to eat. Each story is read by the teacher or parent, with the child repeating and pointing out each feature as it is read. By reading these brief stories, *the child develops a knowledge of, and personal attachment to, these interesting and intriguing creatures -- as well as an appreciation and respect for the natural environment in which they live.*

✸ **The Alpha Sounds.** Each of these Animals has a name that begins with (or ends with, or contains) one of the 43 phonetic Alpha Sounds. At the end of each story, the child learns to derive the Alpha Sound from its corresponding Alpha Animal. ('**frog** begins with **fff**!') Thus, *the child develops a secure association between the Animal and the Sound it represents.* If the child ever forgets a Sound, he/she just recalls it by remembering a familiar Animal friend.

✸ **The Alpha Symbols.** In addition to the picture and story, the page includes the various Alpha Symbols associated with that Animal -- lower-case in the upper-left, capitals in lower-right, and secondary or rare Symbols in the lower-left. Thus, *the child learns to connect the Alpha Sound with the Symbols that represent it. Since all the major Symbols are shown for each Sound, the child won't become frustrated by spellings that might otherwise appear to be 'irregular.'*

ANIMAL ADVENTURE: **The Naturalistic Finnegan the Frog** [facing page]
In this *Animal Adventure* story, the **fff**-Sound is associated with Finnegan the Frog. The child learns what Finnegan looks like ('fat, fast')
what his personality is like ('funny'), where he lives ('Amazon Rain Forest'), what he likes to do (climb to the 'highest branch'), and what he likes to eat ('buzzy flies'). The **fff**-Sound is represented by the letter **f** -- but also [on the advanced page shown here] by the less-common Symbols **ff** (as in **stiff**) and **ph** (as in **phone**), as well as the rare Symbols **gh** (as in **tough**) and **v** (as in **Pavlov**). At the end of the story, the child learns to derive the **fff**-Sound from the picture of the Finnegan by repeating the simple mantra, 'Frog begins with **fff**.'
By reading such pages, *the child learns the Alpha Animals, the Alpha-Sounds, the Alpha Symbols, and the picture-to-Sound derivation process -- as well as the life and habits of many interesting and intriguing animals. He/she thus becomes equipped to play word games like* Phonetic Blocks, *and to read a wide range of basic words phonetically.*

f

FINNEGAN THE FAT FROG

Finnegan the fast, fat, funny frog
lives on a high branch
in the Amazon Rain Forest.
Finnegan likes to catch
buzzy flies by flipping out
his long tongue.

ff

ph **gh**  **F**

Alpha Sounds A2. SILLY STORIES FOR ALPHA SOUNDS:
Dr. Seuss-Style Stories for All 43 Alpha Animals

Silly Stories for Alpha Sounds -- a child's <u>second</u> A30lphabet Book -- is a companion to *Alpha Sound Animal Adventures* (#1 above). It contains zany, Dr. Seuss-like stories composed of words that begin with the featured Sound. The book is designed to help children recognize the 43 Alpha Sounds, as they are heard in spoken language. While *Animal Adventures* focuses on the life and habits of the actual Animal, *Silly Stories* concentrates on words that start with the Sound that Animal represents. Whereas *Animal Adventures* is illustrated naturalistically, *Silly Stories* uses a kooky, cartoonish style to emphasize the odd and amusing Sounds language sometimes makes.

✸ **The Alpha Sounds with Zany Alpha Animals**. As with *Animal Adventures,* each story focuses on an Alpha Animal -- an animal whose name that begins with (or ends with, or contains) one of the 43 phonetic Alpha Sounds of the English language. Each story uses a zany story and a goofy illustration to present a variety of words that begin with the featured Sound. The teacher or parent reads the story, emphasizing and exaggerating the featured Sound, with the child repeating and pointing out each element as it is read. At the end of the story, the child derives the Alpha-Sound from the corresponding Alpha Animal. ('Frog begins with **fff**!) Thus, *the child learns to recognize the Alpha Sounds, and to recall them by way of familiar and easily-remembered animal friends.* Furthermore, by searching the picture, *the child learns the meanings of many interesting and intriguing words -- without lengthy explanations or tedious dictionary look-ups.*

✸ **The Alpha Symbols**. As with *Animal Adventures*, the page also includes the various Alpha Symbols associated with that Animal -- lower-case in the upper-left, capitals in lower-right, and secondary or rare Symbols in the lower-left. Thus, *the child learns to connect the Alpha Sound with the Symbols that represent it. Since all the major Symbols are shown for each Sound, the child won't become frustrated by spellings that might other-wise appear to be 'irregular.'*

SILLY STORY: The 'Phonetically-Funny' Finnegan the Frog [facing page]

In this *Silly Story*, the **fff**-Sound is again associated with Finnegan the Frog. As the story is read, the child encounters much alliteration (21 instances of the **fff**- Sound), some interesting action (Finnegan vs. Felix the Fish), other amusing characters ('five fat, floating flies'), some challenging vocabulary ('phony'), and other amusing details (a fish with 'four flat feet'). As with *Animal Adventures*, the **fff**-Sound is represented by the letter **f** -- but also [on the advanced page, not shown] by the less-common Symbols **ph**, **ff**, as well as the rare Symbols **gh** and **v**. At the end of the story, the child learns to derive the **fff**-Sound from the picture of Finnegan by repeating the simple mantra, 'Finnegan begins with **fff**!' By reading this page, *the child continues to learn the Alpha Animals, the Alpha Sounds, the Alpha Symbols, and the picture-to-Sound derivation process. He/she also receives extensive practice in vocabulary, alliteration, and complex phraseology.*

f · F · ff · ph · gh · v

Finnegan the Frog

Finnegan the funny, fat Frog
fights for five fat, floating flies
with his friend Finnegan,
the phony fish with four flat feet.

Now say:
"Frog begins with /f-f-f/!"

Alpha Sounds A3. ALPHA BABIES:
Cuddly Beanie Babies for All 43 Alpha Sounds

Animals are a major theme running through the entire Animal Kingdom Program. Among other things, the Alpha Animals are used to derive the Alpha Sounds, to combine the Alpha Symbols, and as characters in Animal Kingdom stories. Because the Alpha Animals are so very important, it is essential that they be fully assimilated and clearly remembered by every young reader. In *Animal Adventures,* we make these Animals vivid by showing their appearance, their character, and their habits. In *Silly Stories,* we make these Animals interesting and fun by featuring them in zany and amusing stories. With *Alpha Babies,* we take the bonding process one step further: *We make the Alpha Animals into tangible and cuddly companions -- pets so adorable the child will never forget the Alpha Sounds they represent.*

❀ **The Phenomenon of Beanie Babies.** *Beanie Babies* are among the most popular toys ever made. Since 1992, several hundred different animals have been introduced, spawning *a manufacturing empire of over $6 billion.* The extraordinary popularity of these creatures is due in part to personalization. Each animal comes with a tag showing its name, its day of 'birth,' and a poem or jingle that tells the child something special about the animal.

❀ **Alpha Babies.** *Alpha Babies* are *Beanie Babies* that have been reinterpreted and repositioned in the light of AK's new phonics platform. *Alpha Babies* are plush, bean-filled animal figures that represent the 43 phonetic Sounds of the English language. Similar to *Beanie Babies*, each Animal can be 'registered' for adoption and networked with a community of *Alpha-Baby* 'parents' -- where children can share stories and anecdotes online about their favorite animal 'pets.'

❀ **Alpha-Baby Storybooks.** Much like *Beanie Babies*, each *Alpha-Baby* is personalized with a tag attached to its collar. In this case, the tags contain stories that actually help the child to read. Bright-white tags contain the *Animal Adventure* story for the particular Animal, while cream-color tags are for *Silly Stories. This miniature storybook format is fascinating to young children, so they are motivated to learn to read the stories for themselves, rather than depend on the parent or teacher.*

❀ **The Market for Alpha Babies.** *Alpha Babies* improves on *Beanie Babies* by adding reading instruction to its attractions as a toy. Therefore, Alpha Babies could displace *Beanie Babies* for a substantial portion of its vast market. Furthermore, *Alpha Babies* could substantially expand that huge *Beanie Baby* market in at least two ways: First, *whereas Beanie Babies are bought primarily by families in individual homes, the market for Alpha Babies would naturally expand to the schools and other learning environments.* And second, *because the purpose of Alpha Babies is to teach all 43 Alpha Sounds, the parent or school would be highly motivated to collect complete sets of all 43 Alpha Animals.*[3]

Alpha Babies. Each *Alpha Baby* is tagged with a miniature storybook -- the *Animal Adventure* or *Silly Story* for that particular Alpha Animal.

[3] To complete the Alpha Baby experience, parents will even be able to buy Alpha Baby costumes for their own babies!

B. KIDS COMBINE THE ALPHA SOUNDS
TO FORM WORDS & SYLLABLES

The previous section focused on the fundamental components of Phonetic Reading -- the Alpha Sounds, the Alpha Symbols, and the Alpha Animals. In this present section, we address the skill of *Phonetic Reading itself -- the process of blending various Sounds to form Words.* We concentrate on one key product that enables children to practice virtually every phonetic combination in the English language.

Phonetic Reading B1. PHONETIC BLOCKS:
Over 353,000 Words & Syllables from 13 Blocks

Phonetic Blocks **is the champion racehorse of the Animal Kingdom Program.** *Phonetic Blocks* teaches all the fundamental skills of Phonetic Reading and Spelling.[4] These skills are essential for playing a variety of reading, spelling, comprehension, grammar, and writing games throughout the Program.

⊛ **Phonetic Blocks.** A set of 13 color-coded letter blocks,[5] containing all the major Alpha Symbols on various faces. When selected Blocks are rolled like dice and arranged in the proper order, they form[6] virtually all the pronounceable syllables in our language, and no unpronounceable syllables. Games are sequenced from easiest to hardest combinations, so *each child ultimately learns to decode a repre-*

sentative assortment of over 353,000 different words and syllables. With this preparation, *children are equipped to read and spell virtually any word or syllable they will ever encounter.*

⊛ **Complement, Not Competition**. Phonetic Blocks can be used to prepare students for other modules of the AK Program. Alternatively, *the materials can be used to complement a teacher's preferred reading program.* For example, the Blocks can be used to provide supplementary phonics instruction for a reading program that is primarily Whole Language.

⊛ **Diverse Learning Environments and Markets**. Because Phonetic Blocks is a tangible play material, *the product is especially adaptable to a broad variety of learning environments* -- traditional primary-grade classrooms, hands-on Montessori-type programs, remedial and special-ed classes, second-language instruction, pre-kindergarten learning, tutorial reading centers, home reading instruction, family recreation, and so forth (68). *Along with Alpha Babies, Perennial Favorites and Skirvana, Phonetic Blocks have perhaps the greatest potential to become an all-time blockbuster hit.*

---

[4] In phonics language, Phonetic Reading and Spelling are known as 'decoding' and 'encoding.'
[5] 21 Blocks when including Capitals.
[6] In combination with companion materials called Symbol Strips. (See *The Six Wild Cats Book* [12]).

A POPULAR PHONETIC BLOCKS GAME: STACKS

nge the four
nge Capital
ks in a verti-

'Hat!'

THE GAME OF STACKS

A wide variety of language arts games can be played with *Phonetic Blocks*. This very popular game, called Stacks, is played with Orange Blocks 1-4, Yellow Block 1, and Green Block 1. The Blocks are rolled like dice and placed on a colored Pattern, with the Yellow and Green Blocks positioned on the top row, and the four Orange Blocks arranged in a column ('Stack') to their left.

The young reader moves the Yellow and Green Blocks down the column, reading each word or syllable in succession. Since all four words end with the same Sound, they demonstrate the principle of 'rhyme.'

Play continues for 3-5 minutes, with the student completing as many words as possible during that period. The child writes the words and syllables on individual 'Tickets.' When the game ends, these Tickets are sorted into three piles:

*Real words. Like **mat** and **bat**.

*Real syllables.
  Like **mas** (as in '**mas**-ter').

*Nonsense syllables.
  Like **gat** or **quat**.

The real words and real syllables can be used in stories the children write (see *Write Your Own Silly Stories*, 14). The nonsense syllables can be used in creative writing, where each child imagines a definition for words like **gat** or **quat** and uses them in those same stories.

Ultimately, the collected Tickets will be exchanged for play money, which can be used in the Miniature Economy to purchase special prizes.

By playing Phonetic Blocks games, kids learn the Alpha Sounds, the Alpha Symbols, blending, syllables,

C. KIDS COMPOSE STORIES FROM THE ALPHA SOUNDS

Writing C1. SILLY STORIES FROM ALPHA-LAND:
Zany, One-Sentence Stories for Each of the Alpha Sounds

In sections 1 and 2, we showed how Animal Kingdom teaches Language Art #1, Phonetic Reading. In this section, we combine Phonetic Reading with three other Language Arts: Vocabulary & Comprehension (LA2), Grammar (LA4) and Writing & Composition (LA 6). All these Skills are showcased in an important AK innovation, the Silly Story.

❈ **AK's Dr. Seuss: The Silly Story.** A Silly Story is a brief, highly-pictorial, often-one-sentence combination of story and illustration – in which most of the important words begin with (or contain) a particular Alpha Sound. For instance, in AK's alphabet book *Silly Stories for Alpha Sounds*, the story of Baldwin the Bear is built mostly of words that begin with the <u>*bbb*</u>-Sound – and shows kids how to derive that <u>*bbb*</u>-Sound from Baldwin's name. *AK's Silly Stories offer the same zany amusement as the beloved Dr. Seuss – but with significant improvements: AK's stories are far more phonetically integrated, and therefore far more effective in teaching reading.*

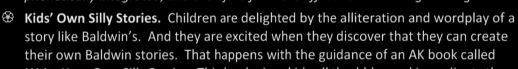

BALDWIN THE BAGGY BEAR
Baldwin the baggy, brown,
baseball bear
buys Bertha the beaver
a beautiful, blue bicycle
for her big
birthday bash.
Bing bong
goes Bertha's bell!

❈ **Kids' Own Silly Stories.** Children are delighted by the alliteration and wordplay of a story like Baldwin's. And they are excited when they discover that they can create their own Baldwin stories. That happens with the guidance of an AK book called *Write Your Own Silly Stories*. This book gives kids all the <u>*bbb*</u>-word ingredients they will need to write such stories: The possible names of Baldwin's parents, siblings, and cousins. The names and animal-types of Baldwin's friends. The various kinds of words that can be used to flesh out the story: Nouns, verbs, adjectives, etc. (see facing page)

❈ **Crazy Examples of Silly Stories.** Once kids have all the word ingredients for their story, they then need some ideas on what story to tell. The AK book *Silly Stories from Alpha Land* gives kids a whole set of amusing examples. *These* Alpha-Land *stories show kids just how wild and goofy a story can get, when it's composed primarily of a single Alpha Sound. It inspires them to use all those <u>bbb</u>-words to create their own stories that are just as crazy.*

Silly Stories from Alpha-Land is a set of stories framed as a Seek-and-Find 'Treasure Hunt' (see 60). Kids pore over a complex, action-packed, funny scene or tableau, to discover all the possible words of a given Alpha Sound that might describe that scene. Then the parent or teacher flips the page to show the actual story described in that scene. Together, parent or teacher and child point out each element of the story as it is read, emphasizing the featured Alpha Sound. The child might then go back and refine his/her story even further – adding new elements from the *Alpha-Land* story just read. As a final step, the child then illustrates his/her story– and displays the final result before the class.

On the facing page, we show you the tableaux for six of these *Alpha-Land* stories for the <u>*bbb*</u>-Sound. *See how many <u>bbb</u>-words you can come up with for each tableau. Then, flip the page over, and see all the <u>bbb</u>-words AK incorporated into each story.*

THEODOR SEUSS GEISEL

The New Dr. Seuss. Animal Kingdom presents zany characters and goofy situations much like Dr. Seuss, but uses words that are far more phonetically consistent.

BALDWIN AND HIS FRIENDS
Bbb-Word Ingredients for Your Story
[from the AK book *Write Your Own Silly Stories*, C2]

Make up your own Silly Story about Baldwin the Bear, his family, and his friends.
Here are some good *bbb*-words:

❀ Baldwin's Family: **Baldwin, Bertha, Buster,** and **Beulah.**

❀ Baldwin's friends: **Bogart the Beaver, Bridget the Butterfly, Beauregard the Bee,** and **Bobo the Beetle.**

❀ Names: **Barclay, Barlow, Bernard, Boris,** and **Byron. Babs, Bethany,** and **Brittany.**

❀ Name-words: **baby, bacon, bag, ball, balloon, banana, baseball, basketball, bat, bath, beach, battle, beak, bed, bell, barn, bicycle, bird, birthday, book, bottle, box, bread, brush, butter.**

❀ Action-words: **bake, bark, beg, begin, belong, break, brush, buy, bury.**

❀ Describing-words: **bad, baggy, bare, big, blue, brown, black, backward.**

❀ Connecting-words: **back, before, behind, below.**

❀ Other words: **bang, bong.**

bbb-words in each of these six scenes: 28, 33, 15, 20, 28, 43. Write down all the *bbb*-words you can discover in each tableau. Then turn the page to read AK's actual stories. How well did you do?

Baboons By The Beach
It's a bright, beautiful day at the beach with blue skies and billowing clouds as a boat passes below a biplane pulling a banner of bottles while a bunch of baboons in berets bury bones, play banjo, and balance on beach balls, as a broken box of bananas brushes by.

The Bull By The Barn
A bear with a book bag, bending a brass bar, balances a bike backwards, beyond the barn, where a big blue bull in a bad mood is busting boulders into bits on a bulldozer, while both big, bad badgers are building their bulging biceps by boosting barbells.

Bat On A Broom
A black bat on a brown broom with a bucket of broccoli and a basket of bush beans blasts between a bevy of busy, buzzy bees and a bunch of bouncing, bobbling balloons.

Birthday In The Bathtub
At a birthday bash on a brick bridge, a bear in a bathtub bounces a basketball, beside a bird with a bell and a big beak, who blows bluish bubbles that burst -- while big, buck-toothed Betty Beaver balances a bluebird with a baseball on her brown bat behind her, when Betty brings back her bitty, babbling baby beaver in a bonnet, who bites a bit of birthday cake from a bulging barrel before her.

Balancing Buffaloes
A blaring band of bearded buffalo brothers balances on bowling balls, while blowing a bugle and a bassoon, and beating a bass drum.

Bear Breakfast

A big brown bored bear in a bitsy beanie having breakfast in bed bites some bacon while a beetle butters his bread with a brush and a butterfly in a bow tie and boots balances a bunch of buttons on a book about baby buggies.

D. KIDS BECOME MOTIVATED TO LEARN

It is great to present students with quality learning materials. And it is wonderful to provide children with dedicated teachers. *But how do we motivate kids, so they actually <u>want</u> to learn? And how do we organize a classroom and control classroom behavior, so that undistracted learning can actually take place? And how do we arrange and present the curriculum in a way that guarantees high levels of success for every student?* *Animal Kingdom* offers three major solutions to these thorny questions – solutions that will work for almost any subject, in almost any classroom: The **Miniature Economy** (38), **Learning Nooks** (40), and the **Learning Loop & Learning Ladder** (42).

<u>Motivation D1.</u> THE MINIATURE ECONOMY
Rewards for Every Accomplishment

The Miniature Economy is a classroom motivational system that that uses a child-size, grassroots economy to encourage kids to work hard and do well. Much like our Adult Economy, the Miniature Economy proceeds in seven steps:

➤ **Tasks.** Kids apply themselves to a set of Learning Tasks (`jobs') during the week.

➤ **Tickets.** Kids earn 'Tickets' for every Task they complete.

➤ **Play Money & Class Bank.** At the end of each hour's Learning Session, the student-run Class Bank exchanges those Tickets for Play Money.

➤ **Personal Bank.** Kids save up their Money in a Personal Bank.

➤ **Shopping List.** Kids compose a Shopping List of Prizes they hope to purchase.

➤ **Store.** When the Store opens at the end of the week, kids buy Prizes with their earnings.

➤ **Party.** Kids celebrate their achievements together in a weekly Party.

How the Miniature Economy Benefits Kids

The Miniature Economy provides a comprehensive and effective motivational structure for a whole range of classroom activities. A rewards program of this type helps children in at least five ways:

- ⚛ **Stronger Motivation.** It motivates kids to work hard and do well.

- ⚛ **Skills Instruction.** It teaches a variety of math and logic skills.

- ⚛ **Preparation for Life.** It sets a positive pattern for future life -- including holding a job, earning an income, and saving for the future.

- ⚛ **Realistic Psychology.** It employs realistic psychology. It is part of human nature to be motivated by both 'Intrinsic' and 'Extrinsic' Rewards. Money is an Extrinsic Reward that has proven effective in virtually every culture in human history. When used properly, that Extrinsic Reward stimulates a child's appetite for the Intrinsic Rewards (below).

- ⚛ **Catalyst for Higher Motivation.** It instills the principle of 'Deferred Gratification.' Over time, the child's need for Extrinsic Rewards (like money and prizes) fades. Such Immediate Rewards are then replaced by long-term, Intrinsic Rewards -- an innate love of learning and a confidence that hard work will ultimately pay off.

Motivation D2. LEARNING NOOKS
Secluded Alcoves for Self-Directed Learning

Escaping the Confines of the Traditional Classroom. In the typical school classroom, even very young students are confined in very restrictive desks for an hour-long period – where they are required to work continuously until the bell rings for recess. Often, the result is restlessness, boredom, and apathy.

The *Learning Nook* Alternative. *Learning Nooks* are comfortable, secluded areas within the classroom -- where spontaneous, non-structured, self-directed learning and exploration can take place without distraction. Typically, these areas are carpeted alcoves spread around the various sides and corners of the classroom. These alcoves can be separated from the bustle of the classroom by low bookshelves or sets of drawers containing the materials needed for that particular activity.

In the AK classroom, each student completes a specific quantity of desk work during the period (their 'job') -- but then is free to migrate to a very enticing *Learning Nook* of their choice. As a result, *kids complete their assignments more quickly, work more attentively and accurately, retain their enthusiasm for schoolwork, and have extra time to extend their learning through self-directed exploration.*

EIGHT GREAT LEARNING NOOKS

Learning Nooks are not just for idle amusement. They are carefully-designed, self-directed learning environments – places where children may spend as much as half their classroom time, and where they may receive as much as half of all their classroom learning. *Following their own interests and initiative, children discover what they love to do most -- and learn through fun experiences how to teach themselves.*

✱ **Story Nook.** Story-related activities that encourage a love of literature and develop the skills of reading, writing, and listening. <u>Contents:</u> *Library of quality picture books, recordings of those books, headphones. Notepads and crayons for composing and illustrating their own stories.*

✱ **Language Activities Nook.** Games and activities that develop and reinforce Language Arts Skills. <u>Contents:</u> *Word games, language activity books, and other language materials – including AK versions of various Perennial Alphabet Favorites (54).*

✱ **Animal Nook.** Games and activities built around the 43 Alpha Animals. *Contents: AK versions of the various Perennial Animal Favorites (56): Alpha Babies, stuffed animals, animal figures, nature scenes, farm scenes, etc.*

✱ **Building Nook.** Activities that develop a student's understanding of order, structure, and relationship -- using with building materials where kids can design, construct, assemble, and connect. <u>Contents:</u> *Building blocks, Tinker Toys, Lego, Lincoln Logs, Geo-D-Stix, K'Nex, etc.*

✱ **Art Nook.** Activities that develop and expand a child's imagination, spontaneity, originality, and creativity -- through art activities such as drawing, painting, sculpting, potting, weaving, and crafts. <u>Contents:</u> *Construction paper, scissors, paste, colored pens, paints, clay, rubber stamps, art pads, hand looms, etc.*

✱ **Science & Technology Nook.** Activities that encourage students to investigate the world around them and to explore the processes by which things work. <u>Contents:</u> *Aquarium, terrarium, container garden, weight scale, microscope, fossils and bones, magnets, batteries, miniature machines, Marble Mania, etc.*

✱ **Let's Pretend Nook.** Activities that liberate a child's imagination and aspirations -- by providing the costumes and accessories kids need to create scenes and stories around their favorite heroes and heroines. <u>Contents:</u> *Dress-up clothes, stage props, period dolls, action figures, etc. Costumes and props for playing out their favorite books and movies -- Star Wars, Narnia, Harry Potter, Snow White, Peter Pan, Pinocchio, etc.*

✱ **School Nook.** Activities that enable students to play 'School' – imitating and reinforcing the learning activities of the *Animal Kingdom* Program by taking the roles of 'Teacher' and 'Student.' Often, a quicker student will spontaneously assume the role of 'Teacher' – to help the slower 'Student' to catch up. *Contents: AK materials such as -- Phonetic Blocks, Animal Adventures, Number Cubes, materials from the Miniature Economy. School desks, blackboard, chalk, writing paper, pencils, etc.*

Motivation D3. LEARNING LOOP & LEARNING LADDER
100% Learning Success in Tiny Steps

With the *Miniature Economy*, we give kids tangible incentives to learn. With *Learning Nooks*, we set up the classroom so that kids will complete their work quickly and accurately. But the very best way to encourage kids to learn is Success! AK's combo of *Learning Loop* and *Learning Ladder* is a teaching method that *makes every child a Winner* – and gives *every child the experience of frequent and continuous 100% Success.*

THE LEARNING LOOP

The Learning Loop is a highly-structured process of Programmed Instruction – a process that literally programs a child's mind to 'think like a computer.' By repeatedly practicing a series of simple and fun routines, kids can learn Phonetic Reading or any other rote Learning Skill (like basic arithmetic) – and perform it quickly, enthusiastically, and with a minimum of error. *AK's* Learning Loop *is teaching method that makes every child a Winner – and every classroom hour an experience in frequent and continuous 100% Success.*

How the *Learning Loop* creates success. In a typical *Learning Loop* classroom, children work independently side-by-side -- each simultaneously playing some level of the same Learning Game. In each round of the Game, each child goes through five basic steps:

Task. Child is presented with an Easy Task.

Response. Responds to that Task.

Coaching. Receives constructive coaching on improving that Response.

Improved Response. If needed, modifies the Response until correct.

Celebration. Celebrates when he/she gets it right.

A simple *Learning Loop* on the facing page shows how this might take place.

A BASIC LEARNING LOOP FOR PHONETIC BLOCKS
Matching Letters to Alpha Animals

Here's how the game of *Phonetic Blocks* uses the *Learning Loop* to teach a basic Phonetic Skill. In each round of the game, a typical 5-year-old kindergartener named 'Sammie' proceeds through a series of tiny, easily-attainable Steps. *After playing this game a few rounds, Sammie will know how to match a particular Symbol (Letter) to the Alpha Animal it represents.* ***

Step 1. **Materials.** *Chart*: Sammie places Sound/Symbol Playing Mat Chart on desk. This Chart shows the 43 Alpha Animals and their corresponding Symbols. *Block*: Sammie chooses the Orange Phonetic Block with the six most common post-vowel Consonants --- the Letters **d, m, n, p, s, t.**

Step 2. **Roll Block.** When the starting bell rings, Sammie rolls the Block. The letter **p** comes up.

Step 3. **Orient Block.** Sammie (mistakenly) orients the Block 'wrong-side-up.' With the Orientation Line at the top, the letter **p** appears to be a **d.**

Step 4. **Write Ticket.** Sammie (mistakenly) writes the Letter **d** on a small paper 'Ticket.'

Step 5. **Match Animal.** Sammie matches Letter to corresponding Animal on the Sound/Symbol Chart. (mistakenly matches the Letter **p** to **Dinosaur**)

Step 6. **First (Mistaken) Response.** When Sammie raises hand, Teacher comes over. Sammie 'shouts out' the corresponding Animal: '**Dinosaur!**' (Whoops!)

Step 7. **Coaching.** Teacher coaches Sammie to correct his/her own Response. ('Sammie, did you remember to turn your Block right-side-up?')

Step 8. **Corrected Response.** After Sammie orients the Block correctly, he/she shouts out: '**Puppy!**'

Step 9. **Praise & Recognition.** Teacher praises Sammie. Marks Ticket with C for 'Correct.'

Step 10. **Repeated Rolls.** Sammie continues rolling and responding until the bell rings.

Step 11. **Rewards.** When the Game ends, Sammie counts Tickets into piles of 5. Exchanges each pile for a Play Penny. Saves Play Money in his/her Bank for the Miniature Economy.

Once Sammie learns each step in this sequence, he/she can soon progress through the entire series at lightning speed – omitting any steps that are no longer needed. Since each set of Steps is so easy, it takes Sammie only a minute or two to complete each round.

Thus, *in every hour of classroom time, Sammie – and every other child in the classroom -- will have at least 20 experiences of 100% Reading Success! Kids are competing against themselves, not each other -- so every child ends up a winner!*

*** [You need not be concerned with the details of these sequences. Just notice that each Step is so simple and easy that virtually any child can breeze through it. Notice also that the sequence of simple Steps leads inevitably to the mastery of a particular Reading Skill.]

THE LEARNING LADDER

The *Learning Loop* (previous section) described the process of mastering a particular Skill. The *Learning Ladder* describes the most effective way to progress from one Skill to the next – until an entire set of Skills is learned. In a typical *Learning Ladder* classroom, children progress steadily in small, easily-attainable increments from one *Learning Loop* Skill to the next. Those *Loops* are in turn orchestrated, so they lead to secure mastery of the desired Reading Ability – in this case, the ability to read a particular group of simple phonetic words. Instruction is highly individualized: *Each child progresses at his/her own pace -- and each continues to experience 100% reading success.*

With AK's combo of Learning Loop *and* Learning Ladder, *kids always make progress, always advance in steps that seem easy, and always achieve significant learning goals. As a result, students develop a confidence that they can accomplish any Task they set their minds to.*

A BASIC LEARNING LADDER FOR PHONETIC BLOCKS
Reading Simple Two-Letter Words

Here's how the game of *Phonetic Blocks* uses the *Learning Ladder* to teach Sammie to read simple two-letter words – words like **at, ed, is, on,** and **up.** To read such words, Sammie progresses up the *Learning Ladder* by mastering several tiny, easily-learned Skills:***

Skill 1. Match Letters to Animals. Sammie matches each Symbol on Orange Consonant Block #1 to its corresponding Alpha Animal. (*Learning Loop* from previous page)

Skill 2. Derive Consonant Sounds. Sammie derives the Consonant's Sound from the Animal's name: 'Dinosaur begins with */ddd/*!' 'Tiger begins with */ttt/*!' [the Letter's Sound, not its Name]

Skill 3. Vowel Block. Sammie chooses the Yellow Phonetic Block with the six most common Vowels --- the Letters **a, e, i, o, u, y.**

Skill 4. Derive Vowel Sounds. Using the same process as Skills 1-2, Sammie derives the six Vowel Sounds: 'Alligator begins with */aaa/*!' 'Elephant begins with */eehhh/*!' [Short vowel Sounds]

Skill 5. Roll Two Blocks. Write Ticket. Sammie now rolls both the Vowel and the Consonant Blocks. Arranges the Blocks Yellow > Orange. Orients the Blocks with the line at the bottom. Writes both Letters on one Ticket: **a-t.**

Skill 6. Read Both Sounds. Sammie rolls and arranges both Blocks. Reads the Sounds of each Letter separately: '*/aaa/*! */ttt/*!'

Skill 7 (goal). Blend Two Sounds. Sammie rolls and arranges both Blocks. Blends the two Sounds: '*/aaa/* + */ttt/* spells **at**!' [Now Sammie can read simple, 2-Letter words!]

Once Sammie masters each Skill in this sequence, he/she can soon progress through the entire series at lightning speed – omitting any Skills that are no longer needed. Whenever Sammie comes up with the wrong answer, the teacher just takes Sammie back to the Skill where the error occurred – and coaches Sammie on how to correct his/her own mistake.

With the Learning Ladder, children always make progress, always advance in steps that seem easy, always correct their own mistakes, and always end up with 100% Reading Success. As a result, children develop the confidence that they can accomplish any task they set their minds to.

*** [You need not be concerned with the details of these sequences. Just notice that each Step is so simple and easy that virtually any child can breeze through it. Notice also that the sequence of simple Steps leads inevitably to the mastery of a particular Reading Skill.]

E. TEACHERS & PARENTS GUIDE KIDS' LEARNING

Teachers E1. THE PEACEABLE KINGDOM BOOK
Fundamental Principles of All 7 Language Arts

THE PEACEABLE KINGDOM BOOK
The Fundamental Principles of
Language Arts in the Early Grades

HUGH MARTIN
AMALIA KAYE MARTIN

The *Peaceable Kingdom Book* is a comprehensive overview of the Fundamental Principles of all seven Language Arts – along with the instructional methods and materials needed to implement those principles. The AK Program is built upon an array of Fundamental Principles of Learning. A selection of 13 Principles not discussed elsewhere in this book are displayed below -- and are contrasted to typical modes of instruction:

SKILLS LEARNING & CREATIVE LEARNING

The typical approach: Some language programs (including much so-called 'Whole Language') attempt to teach mechanical skills like Phonetic Reading spontaneously and opportunistically, as if they were innate. This is like trying to teach multiplication by randomly exposing kids to an assortment of numbers.

The AK approach: The AK Program makes a clear distinction between Skills Learning and Creative Learning. AK teaches skills like Phonetic Reading explicitly and systematically, using a carefully-structured sequence of games and activities built around the Learning Loop and the Learning Ladder (42). AK then uses this solid, secure foundation of skills as the basis for spontaneous and intuitive Language Arts activities that emphasize Creative Learning.

MOTIVATION & INCENTIVES

The typical approach: Most Language Arts programs have no systematic and comprehensive methods of stimulating and inspiring student motivation. As a result, many students become bored, confused, and easily distracted.

The AK approach: The AK Program consciously applies a broad range of highly-effective motivational techniques to encourage students to work hard and do well. As a result, students are excited and engaged. They learn more and retain more.

RACES & CONSTRUCTIVE COMPETITION

The typical approach: Some teachers avoid competition, wrongly assuming it damages self-esteem by making some students feel like losers. Other teachers stage competitions where only a handful of top students ever win.

The AK approach: In the AK Program, Races are used to build speed and accuracy in an atmosphere of high enthusiasm and focused attention. The Competition is Constructive because it encourages students to top their own marks and improve their own skills -- rather than beating out others. Every student receives frequent praise and rewards, so each feels like a winner.

EMBODIED PRINCIPLES

The typical approach: Many Language Arts programs keep their underlying principles very simple, so students and teachers will not become confused. However, such programs tend to be shallow and limited in the amount of knowledge they can convey. Other programs present their principles as abstract 'rules' that can be confusing and difficult to remember.

The AK approach: The AK Program is built on Principles that are relatively complex. However, those Principles are embodied in interesting materials and exciting games that are easy to use and fun to play. As a result, both students and teachers absorb these complex Principles intuitively and effortlessly, as they progress through the various modules of the Program.

SILLY STORIES FOR ALPHA-SOUNDS

Felix the Frog
Felix the funny, fat Frog
fights for five fat, floating flies
with his friend Finnegan,
the phony fish with four flat feet.
Now say:
"Frog begins with /f-f-f/!"

MULTIPLE MODES OF LEARNING

The typical approach: Many Language Arts programs are based primarily on printed materials, like basal readers and workbooks. Such dry, one-dimensional materials stifle the curiosity and enthusiasm of eager

students. Likewise, such materials cause boredom and confusion among slower students – students who would be capable of learning if taught in other ways.

The AK approach: The AK Program employs a broad variety of learning modes to reach all types of learners. As a result, more students succeed -- and learning becomes more interesting, more engaging, and more fun.

LEARNING INTEGRATION

The typical approach: In some Language programs, skills are reinforced by tedious repetition and boring memorization. Individual Skills are often taught in isolation, with little overlap or mutual reinforcement.

The AK approach: The AK Program teaches lessons from the various Language Arts in parallel. Topics in Reading, Spelling, Grammar, etc. complement and reinforce each other.

PHONICS VS. WHOLE LANGUAGE

BABOONS BY THE BEACH
It's a bright, beautiful day at the beach with blue skies and billowing clouds as a boat passes below a biplane pulling a banner of bottles while a bunch of baboons in berets bury bones, play banjo, and balance on beach balls, as a box of bananas floats by.

The typical approach: Some reading programs concentrate on Decoding and Phonics, while minimizing the subtle meaning and literary appreciation to be found in Whole Language. Other programs emphasize Whole Language at the expense of Phonics.

The AK approach: The AK Program emphasizes both Phonics (Phonetic Reading) and Whole Language (Vocabulary & Comprehension) -- and considers both equally essential to the skill of reading. In AK's view, there need be no conflict between Phonics and Whole Language.

INDIVIDUALIZED & PERSONALIZED INSTRUCTION

The typical approach: In an effort to meet each student's needs, the teacher may employ any of three strategies – often with doubtful results:

❀ *Entire class.* If the teacher teaches the class as a whole, quick students are likely to become bored, and slow students can be left in the dark.

❀ *Groups.* If the teacher breaks the class into groups, students can quickly become typecast as either fast or slow. When there are several groups, the teacher's attention is spread very thin.

❀ *Individualized instruction.* If the teacher tries to teach each student individually, most students receive far too little attention. If individualized instruction is aided by computers, learning can become mechanized and impersonal.

The AK approach: **The AK Program personalizes and individualizes instruction wherever possible -- using specialized learning techniques such as the Learning Loop, the Learning Ladder, Races & Constructive Competition, the Miniature Economy, Learning Nooks, Multiple Modes of Learning, Random Selection, and Seek-and-Find.**  **Although students may all be working on similar activities, they all progress at their own pace, with their own individualized set of Language tasks to unravel. Each receives frequent confirmation the progress he/she is making. As a result, no slow student feels left behind, and no eager student is restrained from galloping ahead.**

REFERENCE & DERIVATION, NOT MEMORY

The typical approach: Teachers often rely far too much on drill and rote memorization. Such learning dampens a student's enthusiasm, strains a student's retention capacities, and leads to random guessing and nonsensical mistakes.

The AK approach: In the AK Program, information can often be derived from a readily-accessible source (wall chart, playing mat, etc.). Through repeated practice, a student automatically commits this derived information to memory, as a way of saving time and effort. Memorization of this type is far more secure and reliable -- since it recalls not just the information, but also the process by which the information has been obtained.

RANDOM SELECTION, NOT LINEAR PROGRESSION

The typical approach: Many Reading and Language Arts programs are based on Linear Progression. They progress lock-step through a series of tedious reading selections, laborious vocabulary lists, and mind-numbing workbook pages. As a result, slow students are often left behind, and quick students become bored and stultified.

The AK approach: Where appropriate, the AK Program uses Random Selection to select a representative assortment of reading passages or other Language tasks. By this method, your student learns not just the specific words in a particular story, but all the words of a given type. Moreover, the interesting and unusual words generated by Random Selection inject an element of surprise and novelty, which amuses and delights young learners.

ORDER & HARMONY

The typical approach: Many classrooms maintain order by confining students to rigid desks and burdening them with tedious assignments. In such environments, students can become restless and hyperactive – stressed out because inappropriate learning methods leave them bored, frustrated, and confused. Other classrooms allow lots of freedom, but offer students inadequate guidance on how best to use their time.

The AK approach: The AK Program combines Order & Harmony with creative freedom. Students' time is structured so that they: a) always have something interesting and worthwhile to do, b) always succeed at what they are doing, c) always have someplace fun and instructive to go when they finish their work, and d) always receive recognition and rewards for their accomplishments. As a result, students learn their basic skills, but also have opportunities to develop their creativity.

ENTERTAINMENT, NOT TOIL

The typical approach: Many traditional programs assume that school must be 'serious.' Therefore, classroom activities are often viewed as some type of 'work' – school_work_, seat_work_, home_work_, _work_books, etc. Other programs believe school should be 'fun' – but sometimes entertain children without teaching very much.

The AK approach: The AK Program uses every means possible to make school both entertaining and informative. AK engages your student's attention and imparts important new knowledge through a variety of means: Games, hands-on activities, group interaction, exciting competitions, amusing illustrations, fun incentives, and undisturbed seclusion. As a result, students enjoy themselves, learn more, and retain more of what they've learned.

POSITIVE, COHESIVE WORLDVIEW

The typical approach: The shallow, poorly-conceived curriculum of some Language programs tells children the world really doesn't make much sense. The confusion and frustration produced by such programs tells children their efforts won't be rewarded.

The AK approach: The integrated, child-friendly Principles of the AK Program convey strong positive messages to children regarding the world they are about to enter:

- ❈ *The world makes sense.* **It has an underlying order and purpose.**
- ❈ *The world is also fair.* **Sustained effort is likely to result in continuing success.**

This constructive attitude paves the way to future success in school and happiness in later life.

F. ADULTS PLAY WORD GAMES DERIVED FROM ANIMAL KINGDOM

Animal Kingdom is not just for kids. Virtually any language-related game or activity for older children or adults can be reinterpreted, revitalized, and improved by converting it to the Animal Kingdom platform.[7] A prime example is the famous game of *Scrabble*.

Adult Games F1. SKIRVANA:
Medieval Mystic Journey to Crossword Enlightenment

The Fame of Scrabble. *Scrabble* is the most popular word game in the world. In the United States alone, one in every three households owns at least one game of *Scrabble*. Over 150 million *Scrabble* sets have been sold in 121 countries and 23 different languages. The popularity of online versions of *Scrabble* and its spinoffs now far exceeds the physical board game. Facebook's online *Scrabble* knockoff, *Words With Friends*, attracts over 13 million players each month. On a daily basis, over 1.6 million participants play that game, averaging over an hour of playing time.

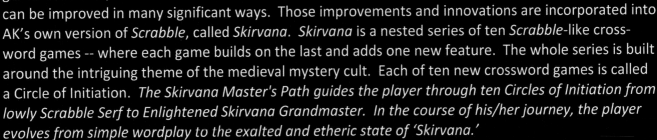

The Skirvana Path of Enlightenment. *Scrabble* is a great word game. However, *Scrabble* has been around for over 70 years, and can be improved in many significant ways. Those improvements and innovations are incorporated into AK's own version of *Scrabble*, called *Skirvana*. *Skirvana* is a nested series of ten *Scrabble*-like crossword games -- where each game builds on the last and adds one new feature. The whole series is built around the intriguing theme of the medieval mystery cult. Each of ten new crossword games is called a Circle of Initiation. *The Skirvana Master's Path guides the player through ten Circles of Initiation from lowly Scrabble Serf to Enlightened Skirvana Grandmaster. In the course of his/her journey, the player evolves from simple wordplay to the exalted and etheric state of 'Skirvana.'*

How Skirvana Differs from Scrabble. Perhaps the greatest fundamental difference between *Skirvana* and *Scrabble* is the Letter Tiles: *Instead of using the 26 letters of the Traditional Alphabet to form words, Skirvana builds words from the many different Alpha Symbols associated with AK's 43-Sound Phonetic Alphabet.* Thus, with *Skirvana*, there is not only a Tile for the consonant **c** -- but also Tiles for the consonants **ck** and **ch**. Likewise, there not only a Tile for the vowel **a** -- but also Tiles for the vowels **ay** and **aw**. All told, *Skirvana offers over 60 differ-ent Tiles, instead of the 26 Tiles of Scrabble.*

How Skirvana improves on Scrabble. *Skirvana* modifies and improves on Scrabble in a variety of other ways. Firstly, *Skirvana offers numerous forms of strateg* not available in Scrabble. For instance, tiles are color-

The Challenge of Skirvana
Instead of just the 26 Letters of the Traditional Alphabet, *Skirvana* tiles include the over 60 different Letters and Symbols of the Phonetic Alphabet. Each tile is color-coded as to difficulty and vowel-or-consonant. All these improvements give *Skirvana* word chal-

[7] For examples, see *Perennial Word Game Favorites* (61).

coded with level of difficulty -- so players can intentionally draw tiles with greater difficulty, and thus greater point value. Likewise, tiles are also color-coded as either consonants or vowels -- so players draw the types of tiles that will more easily help them form words. Secondly, *Skirvana avoids two of the most annoying limitations of Scrabble: 1) Gridlock: The tendency of the Scrabble board to become blocked or congested, so that few interesting plays are possible; and 2) Boredom: Prolonged periods of inactivity (for instance, when waiting for a partner to play) and the relative rarity of really interesting scoring situations.*

The Challenges of Skirvana. The ten games of *Skirvana* increase gradually in complexity and diffi-culty. At the beginning levels, *Skirvana* is much simpler than *Scrabble* -- and provides valuable lessons to young learners in reading, spelling, and vocabulary. At advanced levels, *Skirvana* is far more difficult than *Scrabble* -- and offers mind-boggling challenges in word knowledge and strategic thinking. There-fore, at *some level of play, Skirvana is suitable for everyone from beginning learners to rabid word-game fanatics.*

Diverse Learning Environments and Markets. *Skirvana* can be played as a board game, as software, or through an online gaming community (like the fabulously successful *Words With Friends*). It is *especially adaptable to a wide variety of recreational and learning environments* -- family recrea-tion, traditional upper-grade and high school classrooms, and college & adult game competitions. *Skir-vana capitalizes on the immense and continuing popularity of Scrabble, and injects it with a new set of challenges and attractions. Along with Alpha Babies, Perennial Favorites and Phonetic Blocks, Skirvana has perhaps the greatest potential to become a blockbuster hit and an all-time Perennial Favorite.*

THE HIDDEN WISDOM OF SKIRVANA
Secrets of Becoming a Skirvana Grand Master

Nirvana: State of Bliss attained when we reach the highest levels of Enlightenment.
Skirvana: State of Bliss attained when we transcend every vestige of our Scrabble Ego.

*Skirvana is a set of Crossword Games that lead you through 10 Circles of Initiation --
From lowly Scrabble Serf to Enlightened Grand Master.
By following the Master's Path, you will evolve from Simple Wordplay
To the exalted and etheric State of Skirvana.*

Skirvana Crossword Games
THE TEN CIRCLES OF INITIATION

This ancient codex teaches everything you'll need to play *Skirvana* –
The concepts, the materials, the rules, the strategies.
Most important, it reveals the hidden secrets of
the Ten Circles of Initiation -- steps through which you will rise
from lowly Scrabble Serf to exalted Skirvana Grand Master.

Circle 1: SCRABBLE, The Wisdom of Letters. Here, as a **Serf**, you learn of the 26 shapes we call **Letters**, and combine them to form meaningful words.

Circle 2: SKRYMBOL, the Wisdom of Symbols. Here, as a **Yeoman**, you discover that **Symbols**, not Letters, are the basic elements in words.

Circle 3: SKRABULARY, the Wisdom of Vocabulary. Here, as a **Monk**, you discover **Meanings** of complex words that were previously dark and obscure.

Circle 4: SKARALLEL, The Wisdom of Parallels. Here, as an **Artisan**, you learn of **Parallels** -- the skill of placing two words parallel and adjacent, so that each intersection also forms a word.

Circle 5: SKREAMIUM, the Wisdom of Premiums. Here, as a **Merchant**, you learn of **Premiums** – the many ways a word can be scored as a multiple of its Point Value.

Circle 6: SKRYPOD, The Wisdom of Pods. Here, as a **Knight**, you learn of the **Pod** -- the nucleus of a new Crossword, that can be started anywhere on the Game Board.

Circle 7: SKRANIMAL, The Wisdom of Sounds. Here, as a **Lord**, you learn of the **Alpha Animals** – Animals that represent the 43 different Sounds we use to form spoken words.

Circle 8: SKRALOM, The Wisdom of Slams. Here, as a **King**, you learn of the **Slam** -- a word that earns escalating bonuses by using most or all of the Tiles on your Rack (or even additional Tiles drawn from the Pool!).

Circle 9: SKRAMBLE, The Wisdom of Transformations. Here, as a **Wizard**, you learn of the **Skramble** -- a new word formed from a previously-played word, by rearranging Tiles and adding new Tiles from your Rack.

Circle 10: SKIRVANA, the Wisdom of the Grand Master. Here, as an **Enlightened Being**, you combine all the **Wisdoms** gained on your ascending Path – **Letters**, **Symbols**, **Meanings**, **Parallels**, **Premiums**, **Pods**, **Sounds**, **Slams**, and **Transformations** – to form words undreamed of by the mere Scrabble Serf.

THE MIDDLE WAY. To become a Skirvana Grand Master, ascend humbly but confidently through each Circle of Initiation. Never hold your head too low – by failing to take up the challenge of the next Circle. Never hold your head too high – by rushing ahead to Wisdom you are yet not ready for. Instead, take the Middle Way. Draw all the Wisdom you can from each Circle before moving forward to the next.

THE SKIRVANA GAMEBOARD & PLAYING TILES

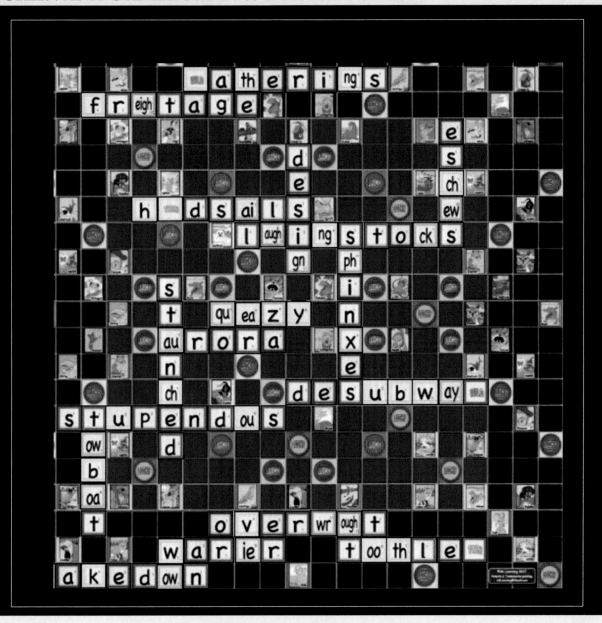

A CHAMPION-LEVEL GAME OF SKIRVANA

When you take a deep dive into this *Skirvana* gameboard, you will discover the many ways *Skirvana* out-shines *Scrabble*. *First*, most of the words played on this board are huge – far longer and more complex than any even possible with *Scrabble*. *Second*, many of those huge words use Symbol Tiles that contain more than one letter – which makes those words longer still. *Third*, many of those big words are completed using several of 16 kinds of Wild Tiles. *Fourth*, there are four separate Crosswords on this board, each with its own big words. *** The gameboard itself is just as unusual. *First*, there are two fields of play – a smaller 15x15 Inner Board, comparable to a standard *Scrabble* board – and a larger 20x20 Outer Board, comparable to *Super Scrabble*. *Second*, the board displays four kinds of Premium Squares – some marked Lucky, to indicate their scores can be boosted even further by a roll of the dice. *Third*, there are pictures of the Alpha Animals scattered all over the board – indicating that players will receive extra scores, when
the Alpha Sound in the word they play covers an Animal with the same Alpha Sound. *** These are just a

G. Projects Under Development
From Animal Kingdom

Animal Kingdom continues to develop numerous other Language Arts products. Among those are three full product lines with exceptional income and impact potential: *Perennial Alphabet Favorites* (this page), *Perennial Animal Favorites* (56), and *Perennial Word Game Favorites* (58). Along with one other series of picture books that make vocabulary far more fun and informative: *Big Word Treasure Hunt* (60).

Perennial Favorites. Perennial Favorites are products that are popular year-after-year and from one generation to the next. *The AK versions of these Favorites will have a receptive audience, since they are derived from time-tested toys, games, and materials that parents and teachers already know and trust. They will tend to supplant Traditional Alphabet products, because they are demonstrably more effective in teaching reading and other language arts.*

Projects G1. Perennial Alphabet Favorites:
Converting Traditional Alphabet Books & Toys to the Phonetic Alphabet

An entire industry has been built around a vast array of products that teach children the Letters of the Alphabet. However, *such products can be tragically misleading to children, since they imply that the 26 Alphabet letters represent all the Sounds of the English language.*[8] In fact, according to prominent reading scholars such as Dr. Diana McGuinness, *teaching the Alphabet letters can actually mislead children and interfere with the process of learning to read.*[9]

Animal Kingdom is replacing products based on the faulty 26-letter Traditional Alphabet with analogous products using the complete 43-Sound Phonetic Alphabet. These products provide the proper foundation for further reading instruction. Through Phonetic Alphabet products, *publishers will make a major contribution to successful reading,* and *will benefit from the rejuvenation of several of the world's most popular and proven product lines.*

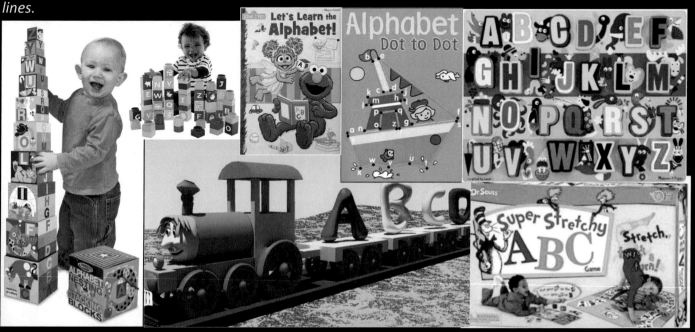

---

[8] For a more detailed comparison between the Traditional Alphabet and AK's Phonetic Alphabet, see page 23.

[9] For studies by reading expert Dr. Diane McGuinness, whose work substantiates the principles of the Program, see Validation Section (73)..

A CAVALCADE OF PERENNIAL ALPHABET FAVORITES

Some of the world's best-loved and most popular children's products are the *Perennial Alphabet Favorites*, shown below. *To maximize every child's chances for reading success, AK is converting them from the faulty, 26-letter Traditional Alphabet to AK's phonetically-correct, 43-Sound Phonetic Alphabet.*

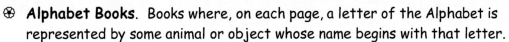

- **Alphabet Books.** Books where, on each page, a letter of the Alphabet is represented by some animal or object whose name begins with that letter.
- **Alphabet Coloring Books.** Books where, on each page, the child colors in a picture that represents a particular Alphabet letter.
- **Seek-and-Find Alphabet Books.** Books where, on each page, a child discovers multiple animals or objects whose names begin with a particular Alphabet letter.
- **Connect-the-Dots Alphabet Books.** Books where, on each page, the child connects dots to form a picture that represents a particular Alphabet letter.
- **Alphabet Charts.** Wall reference charts, mats, rugs, or blankets -- where each letter of the Alphabet is represented by some animal or object whose name begins with that letter.
- **Alphabet Wall Decorations.** Posters or wallpaper whose theme is the letters of the Alphabet (and their corresponding pictures).
- **Alphabet Blocks.** Wooden or plastic blocks, where each side is printed or engraved with a letter of the Alphabet -- and sometimes with a picture that represents that letter.
- **Nested Alphabet Blocks.** Cardboard or wooden blocks of increasing size, that stack or nest within one another, where each side is printed with a letter of the Alphabet.
- **Alphabet Box Blocks.** Oversize cardboard blocks (sometimes as large as a one-foot cube), where each side is printed with a letter of the Alphabet (and corresponding picture).
- **Alphabet Block Books.** A set of 26 miniature books, where each book tells a story based on a particular letter of the Alphabet.
- **Alphabet Puzzles.** Simple puzzles where the pieces fit together to form the Alphabet.
- **Alphabet Magnets, Stickers, Cookie Cutters.** Magnets, stickers, or cookie cutters in the shape of, or depicting, letters of the Alphabet.
- **Alphabet Trains.** Wooden, plastic, puzzle-, or ride-able toy trains, where each car (or section) represents or contains items for one letter of the Alphabet.
- **Alphabet Board Games.** Board games like *Anagrams*, *Lotto*, *Bingo*, or *Scrabble* that are built on the letters of the Alphabet.
- **Alphabet Dice Games.** Games like *Spill-and-Spell* that use letter dice to form words.
- **Alphabet Media.** Recorded songs, videos, and software that teach children the letters of the Alphabet. Alphabet electronic light-and-sound box. TV shows

ples of traditional Alphabet Books
verted to AK's Phonetic Alph

& Write Through Play'

Projects G2. PERENNIAL ANIMAL FAVORITES:
Converting Traditional Animal Toys & Books to the Alpha Animals

Another entire industry has been built around the vast array of products that capitalize on a child's innate love of animals. We call these products *Perennial Animal Favorites* – animal books, toys, games, and other play materials that are popular year-after-year, with each succeeding generation of children. *Such products are appealing to publishers and toy manufacturers, because they will always have a ready market – as each new cohort of young animal-lovers comes of age. These products will receive added popularity and acceptance from the momentum generated by AK's lead animal toy, Alpha Babies.*

Animal Kingdom is converting these *Animal Favorites* into effective learning materials, in two ways: *First*, by assembling sets of 43 Alpha Animals, representing the 43 Sounds of the Phonetic Alphabet. And *second*, by including some enhancement that enables a child to derive that Animal's Alpha Sound from its name.

A STAMPEDE OF PERENNIAL ANIMAL FAVORITES

Another group of the world's best-loved and most popular children's products are the *Perennial Animal Favorites*, shown below. *To maximize every child's chances for reading success, AK is assembling sets of 43 Alpha Animals – corresponding to AK's phonetically-correct, 43-Sound Phonetic Alphabet.* Each of these animal sets will reinforce the connection kids make between the Animals' names and the Alpha Sounds they represent.

❀ **Stuffed Animals.** Plush versions of all the Alpha Animals – not just *Beanie Baby* size – but also miniatures, mid-size huggables, and giant-size.

❀ **Animal Figures.** Miniature plastic figures of all the Alpha Animals – as well as hand-size and table-top size. Along with settings of the habitats in which such animals live: Farm, forest, jungle, ocean, etc.

❀ **Animal Puppets.** Miniature finger puppets of the Alpha Animals – as well as hand-size and stringed marionettes. With curtained puppet stage for performances.

❀ **Animal Jewelry.** Rings depicting a particular Alpha Animal. Necklaces and charm bracelets with clips for adding favorite Alpha Animals.

❀ **Animal Nature Books.** Books describing the Alpha Animals in their natural habitat.

❀ **Animal Story Books.** Stories describing the adventures of various Alpha Animals.

❀ **Animal Treats.** Cookies, candies, and snacks in the form of the Alpha Animals.

❀ **Animal Families and Friends.** Animal figures, puppets, and storybooks of all the other kid-friendly animals whose names begin with particular Alpha Sounds. (For instance, AK's Alvin the Alligator has four brothers and sisters: Angus, Agatha, Anthony, and Annabel. He also has two friends: Ambrose the Ant and Adelaide the An-
telope. All these animals can become characters in stories and rhymes of Alvin's life.)

example of a *Perennial Animal Favorite*, adapted to the concepts and methods of Animal Kingdom. First, *Alpha Babies* come in sets of 43 Alpha Animals. Second, the miniature storybook attached to each Animal shows the child how to derive its Sound. The result is a toy that is already wildly popular. But a toy that will receive added popularity and acceptance -- because it instills in kids the most fundamental principle of Pho-

Projects G3. PERENNIAL WORD GAME FAVORITES:
Converting Popular Word Games to the AK Platform

A third entire industry has been built around the vast array of products that capitalize on the public's continuing fascination with traditional and contemporary Word Games. We call these products *Perennial Word Game Favorites* – Letter Games, Word Games, Grammar Games, Game Books, and other play materials that are popular year-after-year, with each succeeding generation of both adults and maturing children.

Animal Kingdom is converting these *Word Game Favorites* to the AK Platform -- both for recreation and for learning. *Such games are appealing to publishers and game manufacturers, because they will always have a ready market – as each new generation of Word Game players comes of age.*

Letter-Based Games

Word-Based Games

Grammar & Narrative Games

A SYMPHONY OF PERENNIAL WORD GAME FAVORITES

Another group of the world's best-loved and most popular adult and children's amusements are the *Perennial Word Game Favorites* shown below. AK is in the process of converting each of these games to the Animal Kingdom Platform. *All these products will receive added popularity and acceptance from the momentum generated by AK's lead word game, Skirvana.*

LETTER-BASED GAMES

❀ **Scrabble**: Classic word game where players create crosswords using valued letter tiles on an enhanced game board to score points.

❀ **Bananagrams**: Anagram game where players race to create a crossword grid with their letter tiles.

❀ **Spill & Spell**: Players roll the letter dice. Use those letters to create as many words as possible within a time limit.

❀ **Upwords**: Similar to *Scrabble*. But players stack letters to create new words and extend the game board.

❀ **Quiddler**: Players create words from a handful of letter cards, aiming for the highest score.

WORD-BASED GAMES

❀ **Bookworm**: Players form words using adjacent letter tiles on a grid of random letters, while preventing fiery tiles from reaching the bottom of the screen.

❀ **Boggle**: Players find as many words as they can by connecting adjacent letters on a grid within a time limit.

❀ **Pass the Bomb**: Players take turns coming up with words that fit a certain category before a hidden "bomb" timer randomly goes off.

❀ **Buy Word**: Players navigate through a grid of letter tiles, strategically selecting and "buying" letters to form words, while managing their limited budget.

GRAMMAR- & NARRATIVE- BASED GAMES

❀ **Mad Libs**: Players fill in the blanks with various parts of speech to create hilarious and often nonsensical stories.

❀ **Apples to Apples**: Players match nouns with descriptive adjectives to create amusing and creative combinations.

❀ **What's the Phrase?**: Players decipher hidden phrases by guessing letters and solving word puzzles.

❀ **Scattergories**: Players list words that fit within specific categories and start with a particular letter before time runs

ample of a popular *Word Game Favorite* that is improved by applying the principles of Animal Kingdom.

Projects G5. BIG WORD TREASURE HUNT:
Fun & Funny New Words from Seek-&-Find

In Seek-and-Find books, the child searches a very active and busy illustration for a particular character, or for words or phrases from a story or check-list. Many such books have become highly-popular Perennial Favorites -- including the *Where's Waldo* series, the Richard Scarry books, the *I Spy* series, the *Max the Mouse* series, Usborne, and many more. The giant illustration books of Tony Tallarico (facing page) are perhaps the ultimate in Seek-and-Find.

Vocabulary from Seek-and-Find. The 'Treasure Hunt' is AK Program's version of Seek-and-Find. However, Animal Kingdom transforms Seek-and-Find from a mere amusement into a highly-effective learning technique -- employing it systematically to teach giant heaps of new vocabulary words, within a real-world context kids can relate to.

The Seek-and-Find technique is ideal for teaching vocabulary for at least four reasons: *1.) Massive numbers of interesting and unusual new words can be presented with one illustration. 2.) The illustration defines the meaning of those words and puts each word in a real-world context. 3.) For most kids, pictures are easier to remember than words alone. 4.) And for many kids, their appetite and enthusiasm for this game seems to know no bounds.*

...ere's Waldo? Animal Kingdom com-...s the fun of Waldo with the vocabu-...ry-building power of Seek-&-Find.

A 'TREASURE HUNT' LEARNING LOOP

...ere's how a typical *Treasure Hunt* vocabulary game is played, when organized around ...e *Learning Loop* (42):

Illustration. Each child is each presented with a large, complex, and action-filled illustration.

Word List. Alongside the illustration, the child is given a list of words to find, with boxes to check when they find them.

Optional Additional Words. On the other side of the illustration, kids are sometimes given a vertical column of blank lines, where they can list additional words they have found in the illustration.

Word Search. When the starter bell rings, kids search the illustration for words on the list, write each word they find on a separate Ticket, and call the teacher over to point out where they found the picture for each word.

Word Success. When, after any necessary coaching, the child gets a given word right, the teacher marks that Ticket with a C, and gives appropriate praise and encouragement.

Rewards. When the ending bell rings, kids total up their Tickets and exchange them for play money in the Miniature Economy.

...ith this *Treasure Hunt* process, kids become fanatics about learning new words. The ...any illustrations make the words interesting. The illustrations make it easy for kids ...o understand what each word means – and how it is used in context. The Miniature ...conomy turns the words they discover into mountains of 'Treasures.' So kids are ea-...er to learn new words – and easily retain those words in their vocabulary.

Find Freddie on the School Bus Trip and...

- ☐ Barn
- ☐ Baseball bat
- ☐ Basketball court
- ☐ "Clean Me"
- ☐ Dogs (2)
- ☐ Elephant
- ☐ Flying bat
- ☐ Football
- ☐ Frankenstein's monster
- ☐ Giraffe
- ☐ Horse
- ☐ Hot dog mobile
- ☐ Jack-o'-lantern
- ☐ Moose head
- ☐ Pig
- ☐ Pizza truck
- ☐ Rowboat
- ☐ Santa Claus
- ☐ Scarecrow
- ☐ Snake
- ☐ Swimming pool
- ☐ Tennis court
- ☐ Tent
- ☐ Tic-tac-toe
- ☐ Tombstone
- ☐ Traffic cop
- ☐ Turtle
- ☐ Umbrellas (2)
- ☐ U-shaped building
- ☐ Well

Business Highlights
A. HOW AK IMPROVES ON OTHER PROGRAMS

We have featured and showcased many of Animal Kingdom's most interesting highlights. Now let's move on to AK's more general features and benefits. Animal Kingdom differs from and improves on other language arts programs in at least three major ways. Animal Kingdom is: 1) A **comprehensive, fully-integrated program** (this page). 2) Built on an **innovative, new platform** (63). And 3) Implemented through **highly-engaging, new learning methods** (65).

<u>Business A1.</u> COMPREHENSIVE, FULLY-INTEGRATED PROGRAM

Animal Kingdom teaches all seven Language Arts under a single, unified conceptual base. The Program can be adopted as a whole, or parts can be used in conjunction with a teacher's preferred learning program.

✸ **Comprehensive.** While Animal Kingdom places an emphasis on Reading as the most essential skill, the Program combines modules in *all seven Language Arts -- Phonetic Reading, Vocabulary & Compre-hension, Spelling, Grammar, Handwriting, Writing & Composition, and Spoken Language.* There are no gaps in the child's language education.

✸ **Integrated.** Animal Kingdom is *a cohesive, systematic, integrated language program built on a single, unified conceptual base.* Every component supports and reinforces every other.

✸ **Complement, Not Competition.** Individual parts of the Animal Kingdom can be used separately, to *complement a teacher's preferred methods.* Alternatively, the entire AK Program can be adopted as a *stand-alone language arts curriculum that is complete in itself.*

All Seven Language Arts
e emphasizing reading, Animal Kingdom integrates all seven language arts into one comprehensive program.

Business A2. INNOVATIVE, NEW PLATFORM

Animal Kingdom Language Arts is built on a unique, new platform: An innovative set of fundamental language arts principles that *reinterpret, reinvigorate, and improve traditional methods of reading and language arts instruction.*

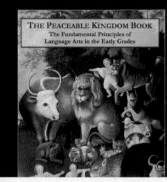

THE PEACEABLE KINGDOM BOOK
The Fundamental Principles of
Language Arts in the Early Grades

❀ **Fundamental Principles.**[10] The Program is knit together by a comprehensive platform of fundamental principles, derived from cutting-edge educational research. Those principles address both language topics (phonics, comprehension, spelling, etc.) and teaching methods (motivation, reinforcement, classroom management, etc.). *These principles reexamine, revitalize, and update traditional methods of reading and language arts instruction.*

❀ **Perennial Favorites.**[11] Many components of the AK Program are derived from Perennial Favorites -- books, tangible materials, toys, games, and activities that children and teachers already know and love. These components are reinterpreted in light AK's new Fundamental Principles -- creating *elements that convey new knowledge to the learner, yet are readily accepted because they are already friendly and familiar.*

A Solid Foundation.
The Fundamental Principles undergirding all seven language arts are explained in detail in AK's *Peaceable Kingdom Book* (46).

❀ **A True Innovation.**[12] Animal Kingdom has re-thought Language Arts from the ground up. It integrates the best new ideas into every component: New phonics principles, new modes of developing vocabulary, new spelling techniques, new ways of approaching grammar, new ways to teach writing, new forms of motivation, new ways to orchestrate the classroom, new ways to make learning secure and permanent. The result is a program that *avoids many of the mistakes and misconceptions that have impeded effective reading and language instruction in the past.*

❀ **Time-Tested Methods.** Animal Kingdom also incorporates the best of traditional and classic language arts instruction -- *methods that have proven successful and reliable, and have withstood the test of time in innumerable classrooms and home environments.*

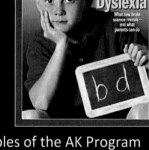

❀ **Solid Academic Research.**[13] The AK Program's innovative principles are built on *solid academic research, thoroughly tested in the classroom, from highly-respected experts and institutions.*

❀ **Promotes Positive, Cohesive Worldview.**[14] Learning to read is generally a child's first formal cognitive experience. That experience strongly influences how the child views the world from then on. The integrated, kid-friendly principles of the AK Program convey *strong positive messages to children regarding the world they are about to enter:*

➢ **The world makes sense**. It has an underlying order and purpose.

➢ **The world is also fair**. Sustained effort is likely to result in continuing success.

This constructive attitude paves the way to future success in school and happiness in later life.

---

[10] For all Fundamental Principles, see *Peaceable Kingdom* (46).

[11] For examples of Perennial Favorites, see 56.

[12] For examples of innovative, new products, see the Highlights section (10).

[13] For research that substantiates the principles of the Program, see Validation section (74).

[14] See *Peaceable Kingdom* (46).

ennial Favorites

Seek-and-Find

Skills Learning vs. Creative L

Embodied Pri

Business A3. FRESH, NEW, HANDS-ON LEARNING METHODS[15]

The Animal Kingdom Program is built on a fresh, new foundation of child-friendly learning methods -- methods where *the joy and excitement of play is combined with a continuous stream of learning successes*. Thus, children learn without toil or boredom -- building knowledge, confidence and self-esteem, while having fun in the process.

⊛ **Fun and Enjoyment.** The Program is built around exciting games and fun activities that engage children mentally and physically. As a result, *learning becomes an entertaining, enjoyable adventure.*

⊛ **Games That Build Knowledge.**[16] Each game is designed to teach and reinforce a particular set of language arts skills. Those skills in turn become the foundation for the next game, where new skills are added. Thus, *as the child plays each game, he/she gradually accumulates a set of interlocking skills -- which ultimately results in a mastery of all phases of language arts.*

⊛ **100% Assured Success.** Most components of Animal Kingdom are designed around an instructional principle called the Learning Loop. The Learning Loop builds learning skills in tiny, carefully-sequenced increments that can be mastered quickly and easily. *Each step is clear, specific, and readily attainable -- so the child experiences a continuous stream of 100% learning success.*

⊛ **Personalized Instruction.** Although children may all be working on similar activities, they all progress at their own pace, with their own individualized set of language tasks to unravel. *No slow student feels left behind, and no eager student is restrained from galloping ahead.*

⊛ **Exploration, Not Regimentation.** The Program uses random selection of reading passages and seek-and-find discovery games to inject surprise and delight into the reading and language process. This approach *avoids the stultifying boredom of lock-step readers and tedious workbooks.*

⊛ **Programming for the Brain.** Children love computers, because computers function with a flawless precision that seems almost like magic. The AK Program *teaches a child's mind to function like a computer* when performing mechanical tasks like Phonetic Reading. As a result, *the learner's attention is freed for more creative tasks, like reading for meaning and writing with expression.*

⊛ **Built-in Motivation.** The Program's games and activities are built on engaging motivation and incentive systems. These include exciting races and other constructive competition, a 'Miniature Economy' rewards system, secluded 'Learning Nooks' for self-directed exploration, and a variety of other techniques that support and reinforce the learning process. As a result, *the very structure of the program encourages each child to work hard and do well.*

⊛ **Multiple Learning Modalities.** Different children learn in different ways. Some are engaged by interesting stories; others like games and activities. Some respond to unusual pictures; others like colors and shapes. Some need to feel things with their hands; other like to engage their whole bodies. To reach all types of children, the AK Program combines a broad variety of learning modalities -- zany stories, funny illustrations, colorful hands-on manipulatives, dazzling oversize wall posters, loveable animal figures, engaging games and activities, intricate patterns and shapes, challenging board games and puzzles, appealing nature videos, intriguing computer games, and much more. As a result, *the AK Program can get through to kids who don't respond to traditional instruction -- such as boys whose small-motor skills are not yet well-developed, or older students who have been left behind by conventional methods.*

---

[15] Details on all these are to be found in *Peaceable Kingdom*, pages 67 ff.

[16] See also *Kingdom of Cats* and *Wildlife Safari* (both 16).

Business Highlights
B. AN OPPORTUNITY FOR EDUCATORS & PUBLISHERS

We have explained what makes Animal Kingdom special. Now let's discuss why the AK Program will be successful -- and who will participate in that success.

Animal Kingdom represents an exceptional opportunity for educators and publishers in at least four ways: 1) **A Win-Win Opportunity** (this page): Ten reasons why Animal Kingdom will be a great educational and commercial success. 2) **Diverse Learning Environments** (68): A dozen major educational arenas where Animal Kingdom will make an important contribution. 3&4) **Diverse Modes of Production and Distribution** (70 +71): Nine types of publishers, manufacturers, and distributors who can participate in Animal Kingdom's success.

Business B1. PEOPLE + PROFIT: A Win-Win Opportunity

The Animal Kingdom Program presents *a true win-win opportunity: A reading and language program that can do much good for America's children – yet offers generous rewards for innovative educators and publishers. In the best tradition of the socially-responsible capitalism, partners in the AK Program will 'do well, while doing good.'* Here are ten reasons why Animal Kingdom will be a great success – both educationally and commercially:

- ⊛ **World's Biggest Market.** At some point in early life, virtually every human being on the planet needs books and other educational materials to help them learn to read and write. Therefore, *reading and the language arts are the world's biggest publishing market. Moreover, new generations of potential learners are continually being born – al* with the same need to read and write. Therefore, products for this huge market seldom become stale or outmoded.

> **World's Biggest Market.**
> At some early point in life,
> every child on the planet
> needs materials to help them
> learn to read and write.

- ⊛ **Broad Appeal.** Because of its exciting games and hands-on materia Animal Kingdom *appeals to a very broad range of learners – primary grade children in traditional classrooms, children in experiential Mon schoolers, pre-kindergarten learners, sub-standard readers in the up dents, handicapped and Special Ed, foreign and second-language students, and many others.* While the AK Program is highly effective with mainstream learners, it is especially beneficial for students who have been left behind or mistaught by conventional programs. (See *Diverse Learning Environments*, 68.)

- ⊛ **Urgent Need.** As is widely recognized, many reading and language programs have failed to meet the needs of America's children. *Inadequate literacy is rampant in our society – and is a primary contributor to social ills like poverty and crime.* Even among more privileged people, inadequate reading and language skills are a severe impediment to future career success, personal improvement, and high self-esteem.

- ⊛ **Recession-proof Market.** No matter what the state of the economy, educating America's children continues to be among our highest priorities. In fact, the demand for quality education increases when the competition for jobs gets tough. Thus, *Programs like Animal Kingdom will continue to thrive, even in a turbulent economy.*

✪ **Support from Washington.** *Political leaders of all persuasions have declared their strong support for programs that improve reading and literacy skills – especially for disadvantaged children and others who have been left behind by mainstream education.* Since quality education is a top priority in all plans for economic progress, programs like Animal Kingdom will receive special attention, and are prime candidates for government support.

✪ **Full Line of Products.** The Program consists of *several dozen language arts products in a wide variety of learning modalities.* These include various kinds of printed books: Picture books, seek-and-find books, activities books, how-to books, teaching manuals, basal readers, workbooks, and reference works. Also included are toys and play materials of various types: Manipulative materials, animal figures, board games, floor games, and construction kits. Included as well are a variety of digital media: Software programs, electronic devices, videos and CDs, and online games. Further included are a broad range of classroom instructional materials: Oversize wall charts, flash cards, patterns and diagrams, and so forth. (See *Many Mammals,* 16)

al Adventures and *Silly Stories* are readily accepted by ...chers and parents, because they resemble the Alphabet ...oks that kids already know ... love. These 'Gateways' in...duce kids to appealing fea...res of the AK Program, and ...t their appetites for more.

✪ **Gateway Products.** Within this broad array of products are several 'Gateway' Products – especially appealing 'marquee' products that introduce teachers, parents, and school districts to the unique benefits of the Program. *As students experience success with Gateway Products, teachers and parents will be motivated to adopt additional segments of the Program.* (See Showcase Section, 22.)

✪ **Numerous Crossover Markets.** Because of Animal Kingdom's diverse modalities, it is suitable for distribution through a broad variety of markets: Educational publishers, educational supply companies, educational and homeschool catalogs, educational software companies, bookstores, toy and game stores, department stores, Costco-type discount stores, tutorial learning centers, educational and child-development internet sites, and online gaming communities, among others. *As a product's popularity is established in one market, its appeal is likely to cross over to related markets.* For instance, after children are introduced to materials like *Phonetic Blocks* or *Alpha Babies* in the classroom, they are likely to want their own sets to play with at home. (See *Production & Distribution,* 70 and 71.)

✪ **Highly-developed Products.** Many of the key components of Animal Kingdom are substantially complete – requiring only final editing, formatting, and illustration. Many other components are fully-functional prototypes. A number of components are adaptations of already-existing commercial products, requiring little further development. *Because development is far along, much of the AK product line can be launched and brought to market in a relatively brief period of time.* (For the state of development of various products, see *Many Mammals,* 16.)

Urgent Need. The ongoing Black Lives Ma... ...ontroversy, and the polarization of Left ... ...ight, are just the latest indications that ... ...ocial fabric of our country is unravelling. ...al Kingdom can restore hope for our your...

Business B2. DIVERSE MARKETS & LEARNING ENVIRONMENTS

Because of its unique approach to learning, the Animal Kingdom Program is *adaptable to at least a dozen different educational markets and learning environments*:[17] Specific learning programs within each category are *highlighted with italics.*

❀ **Traditional Primary Grade Classrooms.** As we have seen in the case of Ronnie, public schools are in dire need of a comprehensive, integrated, and effective reading program like Animal Kingdom. *Public school classrooms.*

❀ **Classrooms for the Disadvantaged.** Animal Kingdom has been specifically designed to reach students for whom traditional methods have proven ineffective. AK's high-energy motivational systems, like Races and the Miniature Economy, are particularly effective for students who feel discouraged or whose attention tends to wander. *Inner-city schools: Schools with high minority populations. Government-sponsored teacher training and placement programs like Teach America.*

❀ **Sub-standard Learners in the Upper Grades.** Because of its appealing, hands-on materials and engaging instructional techniques, Animal Kingdom is particularly suited for children who have been left behind by conventional learning methods. *Remedial Reading classrooms. Peer Teaching. No Child Left Behind.*

❀ **Teacher Training.** Animal Kingdom is a radically-improved approach to reading and the language arts. Therefore, it is likely to receive its most immediate acceptance by young, enthusiastic new teachers -- teachers who are eagerly searching for new ideas and who are not set in their ways. *Teacher training and credentialing programs in colleges and universities. Teach America.*

❀ **Experiential, Montessori-Type Primary-Level Classrooms.** As with experiential learning programs like Montessori and Waldorf, Animal Kingdom teaches language arts through hands-on experience and creative play. For such programs, AK adds important new modes of exploration. *Montessori programs. Waldorf Schools. Traditional classrooms that emphasize experiential learning.*

❀ **Tutorial Learning Centers.** Animal Kingdom is particularly appropriate for private learning centers -- because it offers forms of instruction not normally available in the traditional classroom. Those forms of instruction are particularly applicable to one-on-one tutorial methods. *Sylvan Learning Centers. Kumon Math & Reading Centers.*

❀ **Home Learning.** Animal Kingdom offers the most viable alternative to the Look/Say and Whole Language approaches that many homeschoolers are trying to get away from. For public school outreach programs, Animal Kingdom offers a new strategy for bringing homeschoolers back into the school system. *Homeschool families and networks. Public school outreach programs to homeschoolers. Parents who want to give their child extra instruction at home.*

❀ **Critical Thinking Programs.** Animal Kingdom offers a comprehensive, integrated program that is particularly appealing to systematic thinkers, like those in the Critical Thinking movement. Moreover, Animal Kingdom imbues students of such programs with the analytical and literacy skills needed to engage in Critical Thinking. *Critical Thinking courses, classes, and networks.*

❀ **Pre-Kindergarten Learners.** Because Animal Kingdom is based on experiential exploration and play, the Program is especially suitable for children who are too young for traditional schoolwork. Children are ready for Animal Kingdom as soon as they are able to identify the Alpha Animals by name -- usually around the age of three. *Pre-K classes. Head Start programs. Nursery schools. Day Care centers.*

---

[17] The organizations mentioned in each section are merely examples of a given type of organization. There is no intention to imply adoption or endorsement by these organizations.

✵ **Special Ed, Handicapped, Dyslexic, ADD, Behavioral Problems.** Because of its emphasis on hands-on experience and active play, Animal Kingdom is especially appropriate for students with physical or mental handicaps that would prevent them from learning by conventional methods. With its sure-fire learning methods like the Learning Loop, and its high-octane motivational techniques like the Miniature Economy, Animal Kingdom is especially effective in counteracting the symptoms of Dyslexia and ADD.
Special Education classrooms. Teacher's aide training programs, Individualized Educational Program (IEP). Programs for the deaf and blind. Remedial assistance for dyslexia, ADD, behavioral problems.

✵ **Second Language & Foreign Students**. Animal Kingdom is especially effective for converting students from phonetically-regular languages like Spanish to phonetically-complex languages like English. It is also effective at introducing the complexities of English to students with backgrounds in radically-different, non-Western languages like Chinese, Japanese, Hindu, and Arabic.
English Second-Language (ESL) programs for immigrants. Ethnic Equality organizations and educational initiatives: NAACP, La Raza, etc. English for international learners: Business, government, hi-tech, etc.

✵ **Gifted Students.** Animal Kingdom is not just for problem students. The AK Program will also teach Gifted Students to read and write earlier and quicker. Beyond the fundamental skills of reading, Animal Kingdom also teaches an appreciation for the beauty and subtlety of language itself -- an awareness that is especially welcomed by students with exceptional creative and intellectual abilities. These more subtle dimensions of language arts engage the attention of advanced students -- students who find traditional methods stultifying and boring.
Gifted And Talented Education (GATE). Early learners. Educational toys and games: MindWare, etc.

iverse Learning Environments

Montessori-type Classrooms

You won't just teach a subject, you will teach life.

Business B3-4. DIVERSE MODES OF PRODUCTION & DISTRIBUTION

The unique benefits of Animal Kingdom Language Arts will have their greatest impact on young learners when offered through a diverse collaboration among Producers and Distributors. *There are at least three major Modes of Production (below) and six different Channels of Distribution (facing page) that can participate in Animal Kingdom's success.*

B3. DIVERSE MODES OF PRODUCTION

Animal Kingdom consists of many different kinds of learning products -- reading books, manuals, tangible learning materials, toys, board games, software, online educational and gaming sites, etc. -- each with its own set of publishing and manufacturing characteristics. For instance, the reading books and teacher's manuals might best be produced by an educational publisher; the tangible learning materials by an educational supply company; the toys by a toy manufacturer; the board games by a game manufacturer; and so forth. The components of Animal Kingdom can best be produced by at least three general types of companies:

⚘ **Educational and Trade Publishers**. Many of the printed books and materials of the AK Program -- story books, seek-and-find books, basal readers, workbooks, etc. -- would best be produced by a traditional educational or trade publisher. *Houghton Mifflin, McGraw Hill, Open Court, Scholastic.*

⚘ **Toy, Game, & Educational Manufacturers**. Many components of the AK Program -- such as *Alpha Babies*, *Phonetic Blocks*, and certain *Perennial Favorites* -- are tangible, three-dimensional toys that are best produced by a toy manufacturer. Several other components -- such a *Skirvana* and other *Perennial Favorites* -- are board games or game-like products that are best produced by a game manufacturer. Still others can be made by Educational Materials Manufacturers. *Fisher Price, Safari, Ty Warner, Hasbro, Klutz, Ravensburger, Selchow.*

⚘ **Educational Software & Online Companies**. Because the AK Program is comprehensive, integrated, and systematic, it is especially suited for conversion to computerized instruction and online game-play. *Phonetic Blocks* and *Skirvana*, for instance, would be prime candidates for such conversion. *The Learning Company, Broderbund, MECC, LucasArts Games, Zynga.*

Publishers   tional Publishers

B4. DIVERSE CHANNELS OF DISTRIBUTION

Animal Kingdom books and materials also vary widely in their distribution characteristics. Some are intended for distribution directly through school systems; others through retail bookstores; others through toy and game stores; still others through on-line networks. Although these products come from such diverse sources, and have such diverse markets, *each of them will benefit from success of the others*. For instance, children who learn to love *Alpha Babies* or *Phonetic Blocks* in the classroom will often want their own sets to play at home. Thus, by making Animal Kingdom available in retail stores as well as educational supply companies, *the lessons kids learn in the classroom will be reinforced by their playtime activities at home*. Animal Kingdom books and materials will have the greatest impact on young learners if brought to the public through at least six types of distributors:

❋ **Educational Supply Companies & Catalogs.** Many specialized teaching materials -- like *Phonetic Blocks* and other manipulatives -- would best be offered through educational supply companies. *Learning Resources, Lakeshore, NASCO. Teacher's stores.*

❋ **Parent-Centered and Homeschool Catalogs.** Many Animal Kingdom materials -- like *Phonetic Blocks*, *Alpha Babies*, and Phonetic Alphabet picture books -- are especially suited to one-on-one instruction by non-professionals like parents. Parents often buy such materials through mail-order or online catalogs. *Homeschool catalogs. MindWare. Critical Thinking.*

❋ **Book, Toy, and Game Stores.** Many components of the AK Program are toys, games, and children's reading books. These are best distributed through retailers that specialize in those areas. *Book stores: Children's book and game sections. Learning-oriented toy stores. Game stores.*

❋ **Department Stores, Discount Stores.** The more popular components of the AK Program -- such as sets of *Alpha Babies*, *Phonetic Blocks*, *Perennial Favorites*, and *Skirvana* -- are especially suitable for distribution on a mass scale through large chain stores. *Costco, Wal-Mart, Target.*

❋ **Internet Sites.** Parents and educators often turn to the internet to learn about new educational methods. They will then use the same site to purchase the materials needed to implement those methods. *Education and child development sites.*

❋ **On-Line Gaming Communities.** Computerized versions of *Skirvana* and other AK word games are most easily popularized through on-line gaming communities -- as seen with *Words With Friends*, and other *ls With Friends, Scrabulous, Scrabble GO.*

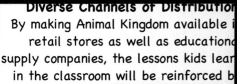

iverse Channels of Distribution

Diverse Channels of Distribution
By making Animal Kingdom available i
retail stores as well as educationo
supply companies, the lessons kids lear
in the classroom will be reinforced b

Appendix
VALIDATION FOR ANIMAL KINGDOM PRINCIPLES

The Most Effective Ways to Teach Reading. Dr. Diane McGuinness is one of the world's foremost authorities on the efficacy of various methods of reading instruction. In these comprehensive, candid, and incisive studies, Dr. McGuinness surveys and summarizes virtually all the major research on reading skills, and explains which concepts and methods produce the best results. These studies confirm the validity and effectiveness of the principles on which the Animal Kingdom Program is built. [18]

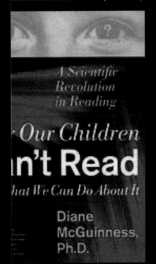

WHY OUR CHILDREN CAN'T READ

"*WHY OUR CHILDREN CAN'T READ* is a superb achievement -- a wide-ranging book that fuses history, linguistics, and psychology with the practicalities of teaching. Its encouraging message is that every child can be taught, if we teachers come to know exactly what we are doing. The book is spiced with well-researched critiques of 'whole language,' of uninformed methods of 'phonics,' and even of an eclectic 'balance' between phonics and whole language -- as well as devastating critiques of several other sacred cows. Some of these cows' may moo back in protest, but this clearly written and authoritative work is <u>the</u> book to read for parents and teachers who wish everyone in our democracy to be able to read."
— Prof. E. D. Hirsch, renowned author of *Cultural Literacy*.

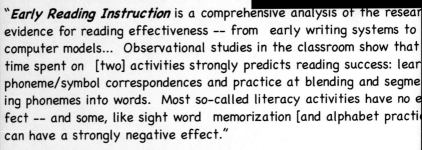

With DK Publishing, Dr. McGuinness has created virtually the only Alphabet Book that is based correctly on the 43 Alpha Sounds, rather than the 26-Letter Traditional Alphabet

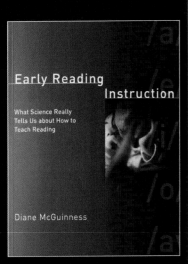

#3. EARLY READING INSTRUCTION
What Science Really Tells Us about

"*Early Reading Instruction* is a comprehensive analysis of the research evidence for reading effectiveness -- from early writing systems to computer models... Observational studies in the classroom show that time spent on [two] activities strongly predicts reading success: learning phoneme/symbol correspondences and practice at blending and segmenting phonemes into words. Most so-called literacy activities have no effect -- and some, like sight word memorization [and alphabet practice] can have a strongly negative effect."

[18] Although Dr. McGuinness does have an excellent phonetic system, the AK Program improves even on that. For instance, the AK Phonetic Alphabet adds the phonetic Sounds /wh/ (<u>wh</u>ale) and /zh/ (<u>Jacque's vision</u>). AK also omits McGuiness's 'vowel+<u>r</u>' combinations -- because the <u>r</u> in these situations actually functions as an Operator, not just as a separate Sound.

Epilogue. RONNIE'S STORY: HOW IT PLAYED OUT

A NEIGHBORHOOD SCHOOL WITH THE BEST OF INTENTIONS

Ronnie's problems began the day Makayla first lead him through the big double doors of Lincoln Elementary School, just a short walk from their rented low-rise condo. Ronnie's family had recently moved to the new Oak Tree Project in West Oakland -- hailed by the Tribune as 'an exemplary model for future urban development.' After kindergarten in Fruitvale, Ronnie was beginning this new school in first grade.

Lincoln Elementary was an older school, with water-stained ceilings and plumbing much in need of repair -- but **not a bad place by the standards of the time**. The school was predominantly Black and Latino -- with a smattering of Whites (whose liberal parents had moved to the Oak Tree to support reverse integration) and of Asians (whose parents often operated the local convenience stores and eateries). **Although each ethnic group pretty much kept to their own kind, there was no overt racial tension or discrimination.**

Learning conditions were pretty good at Lincoln. Government funding had **reduced class size from over 40 to less than 25**, and had attracted quality young teachers from the stellar UC Berkeley credentialing program. Classrooms were often equipped with movie screens and brand-new overhead projectors. Each child had his or her own reading and math books -- a little frayed and tattered around the edges, but still clean and serviceable. Most important, al**though the teachers were sometimes stressed and overworked, they really cared for their students** -- often staying overtime to prepare special lessons for the coming day.

WHERE READING GOES WRONG

The fundamental problem with Lincoln Elementary was not the facility, not the dedication of the teachers, not the lack of government funding -- not even the home environments or the rough neighborhood. Surprisingly, Lincoln School's main problem was actually a very simple one: Curriculum. In many cases, the teachers at Lincoln had been given the wrong idea of what they should teach, and the wrong idea of how they should teach it. Of course, each teacher had her own slant on things, but most their approaches could most charitably be described as '**eclectic**.' Which really meant: **'A little of this. A little of that. And let's hope it all works.'** For the subject of reading, that philosophy of education translated into three major approaches -- all jumbled together in a rather mushy hash:

1. **A LITTLE BIT OF 'LOOK/SAY.'** Like the old *Dick and Jane Readers*, we'll teach Ronnie to <u>pretend</u> he can read, by memorizing what each word <u>looks like</u> on the printed page. Take the phrase 'Look Jane! See the ball!' for example. Let's teach Ronnie that these words are just five different graphic shapes -- shapes he should memorize just like a Chinese ideogram. **This approach will fool Ronnie for a while, but soon he'll run out of memory capacity -- which happens at about 1000 to 3000 words. After that, all Ronnie's reading progress will stop cold, and this happy, confident kid will start to feel really dumb.**

2. **A LITTLE BIT OF 'WHOLE LANGUAGE.'** Now, we'll teach Ronnie to enjoy and appreciate literature, so that he'll be motivated to pick up reading on his own. To begin this approach, Ronnie's teacher (Miss Rose) gathers the class in a circle, where she reads them *West of the Moon* -- with the kids raising their hands to answer questions about what the story means. Compared with

Dick and Jane, this is better! At least these are interesting tales, read with expression, to which Ronnie listens with curiosity and delight.

But as time goes along, children like Ronnie begin to ask inside, how am I to read such stories for myself? Is the ability to read something that will come to me spontaneously and intuitively -- just like a learning to walk? Or is reading a skill like riding a bicycle that I must be taught? Is reading innate, like many advocates of Whole Language tell us? Or must reading be learned, explicitly and systematically, through careful guidance and coaching? **Whole Language gives Ronnie the enjoyment and appreciation of reading, but not the skills he will need to accomplish it. Ronnie now feels a little more dumb.**

3. **A LITTLE BIT OF 'PHONICS.'** Now we'll teach Ronnie the skill of 'decoding' -- so he'll be able to translate all those little marks on the printed page into words he can understand. During the first week of school, Miss Rose brings out a big, oversize Alphabet Book -- much like the *Big Bird* book Ronnie learned from at home. This is a good start! Here are the 26 letters of the alphabet that Ronnie's parents taught him. Here are the 26 Sounds that correspond to those letters -- an **a** for the **apple**-Sound, a **b** for the **ball**-sound, and so forth. How exciting! Now Ronnie can read words like **bad**, and **bag**, and **bat**.

But soon, Ronnie finds that phonetic reading is a whole lot more complicated than he could ever have imagined. Why do we need two letters to make the **ch**-Sound in **chat**? Why do we need three letters to make the **igh**-Sound in **high**? Why does **c** have two different Sounds -- one for **cat** and one for **city**? Why does **a**-Sound have so many spellings? -- one for **may**, another for **maple**, and still others for **mail** and **mane**? Why do common words like **have** and **some** not sound the way they're spelled? Why do I keep mistaking a **b** for a **d**, or an **M** for a **W**? And every time I read **meet**, **meat**, or **me-ter**, do I have to think: 'When two vowels go walking, the first one does the talking.'? **What began as a simple task has now become an arduous and perilous ordeal. Just as with Look/Say and Whole Language, Phonics is making Ronnie feel mixed-up, a little hopeless, and more dumb than ever.**

All three reading methods confuse Ronnie and undermine his self-confidence. On top of that, **none of these approaches are taught in a way Ronnie can relate to.** As a vigorous young boy, Ronnie loves to run, jump, tussle with his classmates, and shout at the top of his lungs. Now he's expected to sit quietly at his desk, keep his hands to himself, and fill in blanks from some boring workbook. And since Ronnie is no longer sure he's doing it right, he is even more nervous and jumpy than before. Ronnie spills pencils off his desk, and teases the girl next to him. His mind wanders to the sunny playground outside, and he often glares at Miss Rose when she asks for his attention. After a while, Ronnie's antics in the back of class begin to disrupt Miss Rose's lessons, and annoy everyone sitting near him. **Gradually, Ronnie is becoming the Bad Boy, the child who 'doesn't know how to behave.'** At this point, **Ronnie's confidence in himself, and in the good intentions of his school, begins to crumble.**

A WHOLE CLASSROOM IN CRISIS

Every student in Ronnie's class began the year with the mental capacity to read fluently. But some begin to falter long before Ronnie does. A few kids begin to slip away during Look/Say: Their little minds are just not agile enough to remember all those arbitrary word-shapes. Or, more likely, their attention span is impaired by a breakfast of cold leftover pizza, or a disrupted night's sleep in a crowded bed. Some other kids fall by the wayside during Whole Language: They have trouble concentrating and following the story. Or they may enjoy the story, but have no clue on how to read it for themselves. Still other kids get lost on basic Phonics: All those rules and exceptions overwhelm their sense of order. Or, more often, those dull, dry workbooks just make Phonics excruciatingly boring.

Before the year is done, as many as one-third of all these bright, eager young kids will be shaken by doubts as to whether they can ever learn to read. And if they can't read, every important door in school and in future life will be forever closed to them.

TINY STEPS TOWARD A RUINED LIFE

During most of first and second grade, Ronnie was teetering on the edge of reading success. But in the end, he was not one of the fortunate few. **There were many factors in Ronnie's demise. But ironically, the major stumbling block was a very simple one: The Alphabet.** That's right: The very same Alphabet his parents had taught him so hopefully through his *Big Bird* book.

As Ronnie knew, there are 26 letters in the Alphabet. Yet, as he dimly began to realize, there are many more Sounds in our language than there are letters to represent them -- actually 43 Sounds in all. So what happens to those other 17 Sounds? What letters or combination of letters represent them? When are there two different Sounds for a given letter? When are there two or more different letters for a given Sound? What special rules change words from one pronunciation to another?

Gradually, all those exceptions and inconsistencies began to wear down Ronnie's mental powers and his self-confidence. Slowing, almost imperceptibly, Ronnie was taking his first steps toward reading failure and a ruined life.

THE FIRST EFFECTS OF
READING FAILURE

Once set in motion, the trajectory of Ronnie's life became increasingly predictable. Even though Lincoln School didn't permit 'tracking' between classes, the internal tracking of Ronnie's classroom placed him in one of the 'slow' reading groups. In

that group, Ronnie found few bright, enthusiastic role models and only rare examples of success. **Once assigned to that slow group, Ronnie became stigmatized by his teacher and his fellow students as a 'dumb one.'** He got less attention from Miss Rose, and what he did get was condescending and pedantic.

As Ronnie's attitude and self-image changed, so did his behavior. Always an active and energetic boy, Ronnie now became volatile, sometimes explosive. To cool off his pent-up frustration, Ronnie was often sent down the hall to the principal's office. Gradually, he became known by other teachers and students throughout the school as a 'trouble-maker.' **As Ronnie became alienated from the Good Students in school, he became increasingly attracted to other Bad Boys -- especially the Bad Boys in the upper grades, the ones who had perfected their 'badness' and had something to teach him.**

THE BAD BOY CULTURE

All those Bad Boys began like Ronnie. All of them had been ground down and discarded by the school system -- a system that told them daily that they were dumb, inferior, and destined to go nowhere. But the strongest Bad Boys had fought back. They created an alternative culture where they could excel. Like Danny Zuko in the musical *Grease*, or the rival gangs in *West Side Story*, or the kiddie gangsters in the crime-spoof *Bugsy Malone*, **these misfit boys would become 'the Best at Being Bad.'** With defiance in their hearts, these Bad Boys actually took pride in their poor grades; in disrupting class; in the knuckle-wrappings they got in the principal's office. They would be the 'best' at: Getting into fights on the playground; stealing the Good Kid's desert from his lunch pail; shaking down classmates for their pocket money; sneaking a smoke behind the backboard; lifting the fast girl's skirt before she could turn around to object; and even at provoking the local squad car to stop and question them. **Before long, Ronnie was a model**

apprentice in the Lincoln School for Bad Boys. And by the time he graduated into Middle School, Ronnie was already becoming a champion Bad Boy, with an adoring following of his own.

THE LIFE TRAJECTORY OF READING FAILURE

At first, Fernando and Makayla were not aware of the changes that were taking place in Ronnie. But gradually the evidence filtered in -- the disappointing report cards; the tense conferences with teachers and principal; the catty gossip from other parents; the hoods and punks that Ronnie brought home as friends. Ronnie's behavior toward his parents became increasingly hostile and defiant. Stern discipline only made matters worse, especially when Ronnie became too big for Fernando to handle. **With deep grief and regret, Fernando and Makayla saw their precious boy slipping into a dark pit from which there was no return. As the years passed, the grief and sadness would only darken into a heavy pall of gloom.**

The rest of Ronnie's life followed an all-too-familiar trajectory. Ronnie went from smokes, to weed, to coke, to smack, and finally to methadone at the county treatment center. He went from lifting girl's dresses; to copping a feel outside the locker room; to sex parties and one-night stands; to the abortion for that slut who claimed he got her pregnant; to an attempted rape he insisted was voluntary; to the life-sapping sexual disease that just wouldn't go away.

Along the same path, Ronnie went from grabbing the Smart Kid's candy; to lifting Twinkies from the local grocery; to breaking into a parked convertible for the stereo; to that bungled heist at the local pawn shop, where he was finally nabbed and convicted. By the same process, Ronnie went from visits to the principal's office; to a night in juvenile detention for drunk and rowdy; to six months in County Jail for minor theft; to **the pinnacle of achievement for Bad Boys: The State Penitentiary -- the Graduate School for Bad Boy Education. There, Ronnie studied under the experts -- the burglars, the safe-crackers, the armed robbers, the con men, the mobsters, the murderers-for-hire -- all the big-time losers.** With that top-flight education, Ronnie probably pulled off some capers that even I am not aware of.

HOW RUINED LIVES END

The life expectancy for Bad Boys is not that long -- probably little more than 40 years -- with much of that 40 spent in jail or stoned out on drugs. In Ronnie's case, life may have ended with an overdose of bad heroin; or a knife wound to the gut from a jealous boyfriend; or the shotgun blast from a rival gang, when he encroached on enemy territory; or splattered against the grille of that huge semi, when he veered over the centerline on the interstate, dead drunk. Or, one chance in a million, he may have lived to a ripe old age, like the Godfather -- romping with his beloved grandson through the tall corn forest of his garden -- until he clutched his heart, toppled, and fell. **Whatever the outcome, the odds for Ronnie were not good. And most likely, his end was not pretty.**

WHY THERE'S ALWAYS HOPE

Would Ronnie's life have turned out better, if he'd only had a good reading program? That would be far too simplistic. But **would a good reading program have improved Ronnie's chances? To that, we can emphatically say, 'Yes!'** In Ronnie's first grade class of Lincoln School, as many as eight kids would fail to become even adequate readers. **With a good reading program well-taught, that failure rate might well have dropped from eight to two.** Moreover, many of those adequate readers could have become good readers. And several of those good readers might have become superior readers. Even more important: **Many of these kids could have been converted from readers who were merely competent into readers who were engaged and enthusiastic** -- readers who read for the sheer joy of exploration and discovery, readers who used that joy to build happy, successful lives.

Let's take these questions a bit further:
Once Ronnie's life was launched on a trajectory toward ruin, was it already too late for him? Was failure by

then inevitable? Or could Ronnie's downward spiral have been turned at various points along the way? Ronnie's chances do diminish as the years progress. But if a good teacher with a good program had intervened by third grade, Ronnie's chances for reading success might still be over 80%. If intervention didn't take place until sixth grade, Ronnie's chances would drop to about 60%. If not until ninth grade, the odds decline to no more than 40%. If not until the end of high school (if he lasts that long), Ronnie's odds are at best 20%. **There are no guarantees, but we do know this for sure: A good reading program will always markedly increase the chances for kids like Ronnie at any step along the way.**

WELCOME TO THE ANIMAL KINGDOM!

So, what is this 'Good Reading Program' -- the one that will improve everyone's lives so dramatically?

In our opinion, **Animal Kingdom is the best reading program ever to hit this planet.** Moreover, **Animal Kingdom is specifically designed to address the reading problems of kids just like Ronnie.**

But that's a judgment you should make for yourself. As you explore Animal Kingdom, ask yourself questions like these: **Is there something very special about Animal Kingdom that could have set Ronnie on the right path from the beginning?** And: **As Ronnie grew older, could Animal Kingdom have been that special lifeline that rescued Ronnie when all appeared lost?**

While you're at it, ask yourself a few other questions: **Could Animal Kingdom have taught Ronnie to read as early as age three -- so that by the time he reached first grade, his future was already secure?** Could Animal Kingdom help barely functional readers like Fernando and Makayla -- sincere, hopeful people who need better reading skills to qualify for higher-paying jobs? **Could Animal Kingdom help Fernando's Hispanic relatives -- immigrants who must convert from a phonetically-regular language like Spanish, to a phonetically-complex language like English?** And is Animal Kingdom only for Problem Readers? Will it also help Gifted Readers to get more enjoyment and appreciation out of great literature? And finally: **Could Animal Kingdom become the inspiration for idealistic, young teachers fresh from their credentialing programs -- the new vanguard who hope to make a real difference in kid's lives?**

Once you have explored Animal Kingdom more fully, we believe you will answer all these questions with an emphatic 'Yes!'.

WHAT SCHOOL MEANS TO KIDS
According to Calvin, school is:
1) A cattle call; 2) An assembly line; 3) A hamster cage; 4) A chain gang.

When you're in school, you feel like:
1) A robot wind-up toy; 2) A parrot that just repeats what it's told;
3) A zombie in a graveyard; 4) A square peg in a round hole; 5) A fish out of water.

Animal Kingdom changes all that!

Made in the USA
Las Vegas, NV
27 January 2024

84971168R00048